“Are you okay?”

She was covered i
whimpering like a
Did she look okay?

“I’m fine,” she lied. “Just a little spill.”

She looked up—way, way up—and somehow wasn’t surprised to find the other runner she had spotted a few moments earlier.

Her instincts were right. He was great-looking. She had an impression of dark hair and concerned blue eyes that looked familiar. He wore running shorts and a formfitting performance shirt that molded to powerfully defined muscles.

She swallowed and managed to sit up. What kind of weird karma was this? She had just wished for a man in her life and suddenly a gorgeous one seemed to pop up out of nowhere.

Surely it had to be a coincidence.

* * *

THE WOMEN OF BRAMBLEBERRY HOUSE:
Finding love, one floor at a time

Dear Reader,

I'm so very thrilled to bring you a new book in my Women of Brambleberry House series! I loved the original trilogy and over the years I've received many requests from readers to return to the beautiful, rugged Oregon Coast. I've long wanted to catch up with the inhabitants of Brambleberry House. It has been a sheer pleasure for me to revisit old friends and make new ones.

I was born in the Midwest and spent my first thirteen years there before moving to the Rocky Mountains, where I've been ever since. My family didn't travel much and when we did it was to other inland areas. I didn't even see an ocean until I was in college!

Once I stood on the sand and gazed out at the vast expanse, I fell in love. I adore the mountains where I live and I'm not sure I could ever permanently live anywhere else, but my husband knows that at least once a year I need an ocean fix of some kind. Writing this book and revisiting one of my very favorite sections of coastline in the world has reminded me of all the things I love about the sea.

Happy reading!

RaeAnne

A Soldier's Return

RaeAnne Thayne

HARLEQUIN® SPECIAL EDITION

Recycling programs for this product may not exist in your area.

ISBN-13: 978-1-335-57364-3

A Soldier's Return

This edition published by arrangement with Harlequin Books S.A.

For questions and comments about the quality of this book, please contact us at CustomerService@Harlequin.com.

Printed in U.S.A.

RaeAnne Thayne finds inspiration in the beautiful northern Utah mountains, where the *New York Times* and *USA TODAY* bestselling author lives with her husband and three children. Her books have won numerous honors, including RITA® Award nominations from Romance Writers of America and a Career Achievement Award from *RT Book Reviews*. RaeAnne loves to hear from readers and can be contacted through her website, www.raeannethayne.com.

Books by RaeAnne Thayne

Harlequin Special Edition

The Cowboys of Cold Creek

A Cold Creek Christmas Surprise
The Christmas Ranch
A Cold Creek Christmas Story
The Holiday Gift
The Rancher's Christmas Song

The Women of Brambleberry House

A Soldier's Secret
His Second-Chance Family
The Daddy Makeover

HQN Books

Haven Point

Serenity Harbor
Sugar Pine Trail
The Cottages on Silver Beach
Season of Wonder

For a complete list of books by RaeAnne Thayne, please visit www.raeannethayne.com.

To Jill Shalvis and Marina Adair.
I love our seaside adventures!

Chapter One

Some days, a girl reached a point where her best course of action was to run away from her problems.

Melissa Fielding hung up the phone after yet another unproductive discussion with her frustrating ex-husband, drew in a deep, cleansing breath, then threw on her favorite pair of jogging shoes.

Yes, she had a million things to do. The laundry basket spilled over with clothes, she had bills to pay, dirty dishes filled her sink, and she was scheduled to go into the doctor's office where she worked in less than two hours.

None of that mattered right now. She had too much energy seething through her, wave after wave like the sea pounding Cannon Beach during a storm.

Even Brambleberry House, the huge, rambling Victorian where she and her daughter lived in the first-floor apartment, seemed too small right now.

She needed a little good, hard exercise to work some of it off or she would be a stressed, angry mess at work.

She and Cody had been divorced for three years, separated four, but he could still make her more frustrated than anybody else on earth. Fortunately, their seven-year-old daughter, Skye, was at school, so she didn't have to witness her parents arguing yet again.

She yanked open her apartment door to head for the outside door when it opened from the other side. Rosa Galvez, her de facto landlady who ran the three-unit building for her aunt and a friend, walked inside, arms loaded with groceries.

Her friend took one look at Melissa's face and frowned. "Uh-oh. Bad morning?" Rosa asked, her lovely features twisted with concern.

Now that she was off the phone, the heat of Melissa's anger cooled a degree or two, but she could still feel the restless energy spitting and hissing through her like a downed power line.

"You know how it goes. Five minutes on the phone with my ex and I either have to punch something, spend an hour doing yoga or go for a hard run on the beach. I don't have a free hour and punching something would be counterproductive, so a good run is the winner." Melissa took two bags of groceries from Rosa and led the way up the stairs to the other woman's third-floor apartment.

"Run an extra mile or two for me, would you?" Rosa asked.

"Sure thing."

"What does he want this time?"

She sighed. "It's a long story." She didn't want to complain to her friend about Cody. It made her sound bitter and small, and she wasn't, only frustrated at all the broken promises and endless disappointments.

Guilt, an old, unwelcome companion, poked her on the shoulder. Her daughter loved her father despite his failings. Skye couldn't see what Melissa did—that even though Skye was only seven, there was a chance she was more mature than her fun-loving, thrill-chasing father.

She ignored the guilt, reminding herself once more there was nothing she could do about her past mistakes but continue trying to make the best of things for her child's sake.

Rosa opened the door to her wide, window-filled apartment, and Melissa wasn't surprised to find Rosa's much-loved dog, an Irish setter named Fiona, waiting just inside.

"Can I take Fiona on my run?" she asked impulsively, after setting the groceries in the kitchen.

"That would be great!" Rosa exclaimed. "We were going to go on a walk as soon as I put the groceries away, but she would love a run much more. Thank you! Her leash is there on the hook."

At the word *leash*, Fiona loped to the door and did a little circular dance of joy that made more of Melissa's bad mood seep away.

"Let's do this, sweetheart," she said, grabbing the leash from its place by the door and hooking it to Fiona's shamrock-green collar.

"Thank you for this. Have fun." Rosa opened the door

for them, and the strong dog just about pulled Melissa toward the stairs. She waved at her friend, then she and the dog hurried outside.

The April morning was one of those rare and precious days along the Oregon Coast when Mother Nature decided it was finally time to get serious about spring. Sunlight gleamed on the water and all the colors seemed saturated and bright from the rains of the preceding few days.

The well-tended gardens of Brambleberry House were overflowing with sweet-smelling flowers—cherry blossoms, magnolia, camellias. It was sheer delight. She inhaled the heavenly aroma, enjoying the undernote of sea and sand and other smells that were inexorable scent-memories of her childhood.

Fiona pulled at the leash, forcing Melissa to pick up her pace. Yes. A good run was exactly the prescription she was writing herself.

As she headed down the path toward the gate that led to the water, she spotted Sonia, the third tenant of Brambleberry House, working in a bed of lavender that hadn't yet burst into bloom.

Sonia was an interesting creature. She wasn't rude, exactly, she simply kept to herself and had done so for the seven months Melissa had lived downstairs from her.

Melissa always felt so guilty when she watched the other woman make her painstaking way up the stairs to her second-floor apartment, often pausing to rest on the landing. She didn't know the nature of Sonia's health issues, but she obviously struggled with something. She walked with a limp, and Rosa had told Melissa once that the other woman had vision issues that precluded driving.

Right after moving in, Melissa had offered to switch apartments with her so Sonia wouldn't have to make the climb, but her offer had been refused.

"I need…the exercise," Sonia had said in her halting, odd cadence. "Going upstairs is good…physical therapy…for me."

Melissa had to admire someone willing to push herself out of her comfort zone, sustained only by the hope that she would grow from the experience.

That was a good life lesson for her. She wasted entirely too much energy dwelling on the painful reality that life hadn't turned out exactly as she planned, that some of her dreams were destined to disappointment.

Like Sonia, maybe it was time she stopped being cranky about things she couldn't control and took any chance that came along to force herself to stretch outside her comfort zone. She needed to learn how to make the best of things, to simply enjoy a gorgeous April day.

"Beautiful morning, isn't it?"

"Lovely," Sonia said with her somewhat lopsided smile. "Hello…Melissa. Hello…Fiona."

She scratched the dog under her chin and was rewarded with one of Fi's doggie grins.

While the Irish setter technically lived with Rosa, the cheerful dog seemed to consider all the occupants of Brambleberry House her particular pack. That shared pet care worked out well for Melissa. Her daughter had been begging for a dog since before the divorce. Skye had been in heaven when they'd moved into Brambleberry House and discovered Rosa had a dog she was more than willing to share. This way, they got the benefits of having a dog without the onus of being responsible for one all the time.

That was yet another thing she had to be grateful for on this beautiful spring day. She had been so blessed to find an open apartment in Brambleberry House when she and Skye returned to Cannon Beach after all those years of wandering. It was almost a little miracle, since the previous tenant had only moved out to get married the week before Melissa returned to her hometown and started looking for a place.

She didn't know if it was fate or kismet or luck or simply somebody watching out for them. She only knew that she and Skye had finally found a place to throw down roots.

She ran hard, accompanied by the sun on her face, the low murmur of the waves, the crunch of sand under her running shoes. All of it helped calm her.

By the time she and Fiona made it the mile and a half to the end of the beach and she'd turned around to head back, the rest of her frustration had abated, and she focused instead on the endorphins from the run and the joy of living in this beautiful place.

She paused for a moment to catch her breath, looking out at the rock formations offshore, the towering haystacks that so defined this part of the Oregon Coast, then the craggy green mountains to the east.

It was so good to be home. She had friends here, connections. Her dad was buried not far from here. Her mom and stepfather were here most of the time, though they had just bought an RV and were spending a few months traveling around the country.

She would have thought being a military wife to Melissa's dad would have cured her mother's wanderlust, but apparently not. They would be back soon.

Melissa didn't envy them. After moving to a new base every few years during her childhood and then following Cody around from continent to continent, she loved being in one place. *This* place. She had missed it more than she even realized, until she finally decided to bring Skye here.

She should have done it years ago instead of trying so hard to stay close to her ex-husband for Skye's sake. She had enjoyed living on Oahu, his home training location, but the cost of living had been prohibitive. Most of her salary as a nurse had gone to housing and the rest to food.

When he decided to move to South America on a whim, she had finally thrown up her hands and opted not to follow him. Instead, she had packed up her daughter for one last move and come home to Cannon Beach.

She started her run again, not wanting to spend more time than she already had that morning dwelling on her mistakes.

It made her sad, wondering if she should have tried harder to make things work, even though she was fully aware both of them had left the marriage long before they finally divorced.

Now wasn't the time to obsess about her failures or the loneliness that kept her up at night.

He had gotten married again. That was what he called

to tell her earlier. It had been a spur-of-the-moment decision and they'd gone to St. Croix for their honeymoon, which had been beautiful but expensive. He'd spent so much on the honeymoon, in fact, that he couldn't make that month's child support payment, but he would make it up to her.

He was coming back to Oregon to stay this time, and was willing to finally step up and be the dad he should have been all along. She'd been hearing that story or versions of it for fifteen years. She hoped it would happen, she really did.

Cody wasn't a bad man. She wouldn't have loved him all those years and followed him from country to country to support his dreams if he were. But with the birth of their child, her priorities had changed, while she was afraid his never would.

Enough about Cody. She was genuinely happy for her ex, even if hearing about his new marriage did make her wish she had someone special in her own life.

She sighed again and gripped Fiona's leash. "Come on, Fi. Let's go home."

An odd wind danced across the sand, warmer than the air around it. She almost thought she could hear laughter rippling around her, though she was virtually alone on the beach.

She was hearing things again. Once in a while at the house, she could swear she heard a woman's laugh when no one was there, and a few times she had smelled roses on the stairwell, for no apparent reason.

Maybe the ghost of Brambleberry House had been

in the mood for a run today, too. The thought made her smile and she continued heading home.

Few people were out on the beach on this off-season morning, but she did happen to catch sight of a guy running toward her from the opposite direction. He was too far away for her to really see clearly, but she had the random impression of lean strength and fluid grace.

Ridiculous, she told herself. How could she know that from two hundred yards away?

She continued running, intent now only on finishing so she could go into work.

Fiona trotted along beside her in the same rhythm they had worked out through countless runs like this together. She was aware of the other runner coming closer. He had a dog, too, a small black one who also looked familiar.

They were only fifty feet apart when Fiona, for no apparent reason, suddenly veered in front of Melissa, then stopped stock-still.

With no time to change course or put on the brakes, Melissa toppled over the eighty-pound dog and went flying across the sand. She shoved her hands out to catch her fall instinctively. Her right arm hit sand and she felt a jolt in her shoulder from the impact, but the left one must have made contact with a rock buried beneath the sand, causing a wrenching pain to shoot from her wrist up her arm.

This day just kept getting better and better.

She gasped and flopped over onto her back, cradling the injured wrist as a haze of pain clouded her vision.

Fiona nosed her side as if in apology, and Melissa

bit back her instinctive scold. What on earth had gotten into Fiona? They had run together dozens of times. The Irish setter was usually graceful, beautifully trained, and never cut across her path like that.

For about ten seconds, it was all she could do not to writhe around on the ground and howl. She was trying not to cry when she gradually became aware she wasn't alone.

"Are you okay?" a deep male voice asked.

She was covered in sand, grabbing her wrist and whimpering like a baby seal that had lost its mama. Did she *look* okay?

"I'm fine," she lied. "Just a little spill."

She looked up—way, way up—and somehow wasn't surprised to find the other runner she had spotted a few moments earlier.

Her instincts were right. He *was* great-looking. She had an impression of dark hair and concerned blue eyes that looked familiar. He wore running shorts and a form-fitting performance shirt that molded to powerfully defined muscles.

She swallowed and managed to sit up. What kind of weird karma was this? She had just wished for a man in her life, and suddenly a gorgeous one seemed to pop up out of nowhere.

Surely it had to be a coincidence.

Anyway, she might like the idea of a man in her life, but she wasn't at all prepared for the reality of it—especially not a dark-haired, blue-eyed runner who still somehow managed to smell delicious.

He also had a little dog on a leash, a small black

schnauzer who was sniffing Fiona like they were old friends.

"Can I give you a hand?"

"Um. Sure."

Still cradling her injured wrist, she reached out with her right hand, and he grasped it firmly and tugged her to her feet. For one odd moment, she could swear she smelled roses above the clean, crisp, masculine scent of him, but that made absolutely no sense.

Was she hallucinating? Maybe she had bonked her head in that gloriously graceful free fall.

"You hurt your wrist," he observed. "Need me to take a look at it? I'm a doctor."

What were the odds that she would fall and injure herself in front of a gorgeous tourist who also happened to be a doctor?

"Isn't that convenient?" she muttered, wondering again at the weird little twist of fate.

He gave her an odd look, half curious and half concerned. Again, she had the strange feeling that she knew him somehow, but she had such a lousy memory for faces and names.

"Melissa. Melissa Blake?"

She narrowed her gaze, more embarrassed at her own lousy memory than anything. He knew her so she obviously had met him before.

"Yes. Actually, it's Melissa Fielding now."

"Oh. Right. You married Cody Fielding, Cannon Beach's celebrity."

And divorced him, she wanted to add. *Don't forget that part.*

"I'm sorry. You know me, but I'm afraid I don't remember your name."

He shrugged. "No reason you should. I was a few years older and I've been gone a long time."

She looked closer. There was something about the shape of his mouth. She had seen it recently on someone else…

"Eli?"

"That's right. Hi, Melissa."

She should have known! All the clues came together. The dog, whom she now recognized as Max, the smart little dog who belonged to Eli's father. The fact that he said he was a doctor. Those startling, searching blue eyes that now seemed unforgettable.

How embarrassing!

In her defense, the last time she had seen Eli Sanderson, he had been eighteen and she had been fifteen. He had graduated from high school and was about to take off across the country to college. The Eli she remembered had been studious and serious. He had kept mostly to himself, more interested in leading the academic decathlon than coming to any sporting events or social functions.

She had been the opposite, always down for a party, as long as it distracted her from the sadness at home in those first years after her father died of brain cancer.

The Eli she remembered had been long and lanky, skinny even. This man, on the other hand, was anything *but* nerdy. He was buff, gorgeous, with lean, masculine features and the kind of shoulders that made a woman want to grab hold and not let go.

Wow. The military had really filled him out.

"I understand you work with my dad," he said.

She worked *for* his father. Melissa was a nurse at Dr. Wendell Sanderson's family medicine clinic. Now she realized why that mouth looked so familiar. She should have picked up on it immediately. His dad's mouth was shaped the same, but somehow that full bottom lip looked very different on Dr. Sanderson Jr.

Her wrist still ached fiercely. "How's your dad?" she asked, trying to divert her attention from it. "I stopped by to see him yesterday after his surgery and was going to call the hospital to check on him today as soon as I finished my run."

"He's good. I was trying to be here before he went under the knife, but my plane was delayed until last night. I did speak to the orthopedic surgeon, who is happy with the outcome so far. Both knee replacements seem to have gone well."

"Oh, good. He won't tolerate being down for long. I guess that's why it made sense for him to do both at the same time."

"You know him well."

After several months of working for the kindly family medicine doctor, she had gained a solid insight into his personality. Wendell was sweet, patient, genuinely concerned about his patients. He was the best boss she'd ever had.

"Let's take a look at this wrist," Eli said now. Unlike his father, Wendell's son could never be described as kindly or avuncular.

"I'm sure it's fine."

"Again, I'm a doctor. Why don't you let me be the judge of how fine it might be? I saw that nasty tumble and could hear the impact of your fall all the way across the sand. You might have broken something, in which case you're going to want to have it looked at sooner rather than later."

She was strangely reluctant to hand over her wrist—or anything else—to the man and fought the urge to hide her hand behind her back, as if she were caught with a fistful of Oreos in front of an empty cookie jar.

"I can have the radiologist at the clinic x-ray it when I go in to work in an hour."

"Or you can let me take a look at it right now."

She frowned at the implacable set of his jaw. He held his hand out and she sighed. "Ugh. You're as stubborn as your father."

"Thank you. Anytime someone compares me to my father, I take it as a compliment."

He gave his outstretched hand a pointed look, and she frowned again and, cornered, held out her wrist. The movement made her hurt all over again, and she flushed at the unwilling tears she could feel gather.

His skin was much warmer than she might have expected on a lovely but still cool April morning. Seductively warm. His hands were long-fingered, masculine, much longer than her own, and he wore a sleek Tag Heuer watch.

Her stomach felt hollow, her nerves tight, but she wasn't sure if that was in reaction to the injury or from the unexpected pleasure of skin against skin. He was a doctor taking a look at an injury, she reminded herself, not a sexy guy wanting to hold her hand.

Melissa aimed a glare at Fiona, who had started the whole thing. The dog had planted her haunches in the sand, tail wagging, and seemed to be watching the whole episode with an expression that appeared strangely like amusement.

"It doesn't feel like anything is broken. You can move it, right?"

He held her hand while she wiggled her fingers, then rotated her wrist. It hurt like the devil, but she didn't feel any structural impingement in movement.

"Yes. I told you it wasn't broken. It's already feeling better."

"You can't be completely sure without an X-ray, but I'm all right waiting forty-eight hours or so to check it. I suspect a sprain, but it might be easier to tell in a few days. Do you have a way to splint it? If you don't, I'm sure my dad has something at the office."

"I've got a wrist brace I've worn before when I had carpal tunnel problems."

"You'll want to put that on and have it checked again in a few days. Meanwhile, ice and elevation are your best friends. At least ten minutes every two hours."

As if she had time for that. "I'll do my best. Thanks."

A sudden thought occurred to her, one she was almost afraid to entertain. "How long will you be in town?"

When he was making arrangements to be gone for his surgery, Wendell had hoped Eli might be able to cover for him at the clinic. The last she had heard, though, Eli's hadn't been able to get leave from his military assignment so his father had arranged a substitute doctor through a service in Portland.

Given that Eli was here, she had a feeling all that was about to change—which meant Eli might be her boss for the foreseeable future.

"I'm not sure how much time I can get," he answered now. "That depends on a few things still in play. I'm hoping for a month but I'll be here for the next two to three weeks, at least."

"I see."

She did see, entirely too clearly. This would obviously not be the last she would see of Eli Sanderson.

"I need to go. Thanks for your help," she said quickly.

"I didn't do anything except take a look at your injury. At least promise me you'll raise it up and put some ice on it."

Considering she was scheduled to work at his father's clinic starting in just over an hour and still needed to shower, she wouldn't have time for much self-pampering. "I'll do my best. Thanks."

"How far do you have to go? I can at least help you walk your dog home."

"Fiona isn't my dog. She belongs to my neighbor. We were just sort of exercising each other. And for the record, she's usually very well behaved. I don't quite know what happened earlier, but we'll be fine to make it home on our own. I don't want to disturb your run more than I already have."

"Are you sure?"

"We don't have far to go. I live at Brambleberry House."

His expression registered his surprise. "Wow. You're practically next door to my dad's place."

They couldn't avoid each other, even if they wanted to. She didn't necessarily want to avoid *him*, but considering she was now bedraggled and covered with sand, she was pretty sure he wouldn't be in a hurry to see her again.

"Thanks again for your help. I'll see you later."

"Remember your RICE."

Right. Rest, Ice, Compression, Elevation. The first-aid prescription for injuries like hers. "I'll do my best. Thanks. See you later."

This time as she headed for the house, Fiona trotted along beside her, docile and well behaved.

Melissa's wrist, on the other hand, complained vociferously all the way back to the house. She did her best to ignore it, focusing instead on the unsettling encounter with Dr. Sanderson's only son.

Eli told himself he was only keeping an eye on Melissa as she made her slow way along the beach toward Brambleberry House because he was concerned about her condition, especially whether she had other injuries from her fall she had chosen not to reveal to him.

He was only being a concerned physician, watching over someone who had been hurt while he was nearby.

The explanation rang hollow. He knew it was more than that.

Melissa Blake Fielding had always been a beautiful girl and had fascinated him more than he had wanted to admit to himself or anyone else when he was eighteen and she was only fifteen.

She had been a pretty cheerleader, popular and well-liked—mostly because she always had a smile for everyone, even geeky science students who weren't the greatest at talking to popular, pretty, well-liked cheerleaders.

He had danced with her once at a school dance toward the end of his senior year. She had been there with her date—and future husband—Cody Fielding, who had been ignoring her, as usual.

While his own date had been dancing with her dad, the high school gym teacher and chaperone, Eli had gathered his nerve to ask Melissa to dance, hating that the nicest girl in school had been stuck sitting alone while her jerk of a boyfriend ignored her.

He remembered she had been everything sweet to him during that memorable dance, asking about his plans after graduation.

Did she know her boyfriend and future husband hadn't taken kindly to Eli's nerve in asking Cody's date to dance and had tried to make him pay? He still had a scar above his eyebrow from their subsequent little altercation.

It had been a long time ago. He was a completely different man than he'd been back then, with wholly different priorities.

He hadn't thought about her in years, at least until his father had mentioned a few months earlier that Melissa was back in town and working for him.

At the time, he had been grieving, lost, more than a little raw. He remembered now that the memory of Melissa had made him smile for the first time in weeks.

Now he had to wonder if that was one of the reasons he had worked hard to arrange things so that he could come home and help his father out during Wendell's recovery from double knee-replacement surgery. On some subconscious level, had he remembered Melissa worked at the clinic and been driven to see her again?

He didn't want to think so. He would be one sorry idiot if that were the case, especially since he didn't have room in his life right now for that kind of complication.

If he *had* given it any thought at all, on any level, he probably would have assumed it wouldn't matter. He was older, she was older. It had been a long time since he'd felt like that awkward, socially inept nerd he'd been in the days when he lived here in Cannon Beach.

He had been deployed most of the last five years and had been through bombings, genocides, refugee disasters. He had seen things he never expected to, had survived things others hadn't.

He could handle this unexpected reunion with a woman he might have had a crush on. He only had to remember that he was no longer that geeky, awkward kid but a well-respected physician now.

In comparison to everything he had been through in the last few years—and especially the horror of six months ago that he was still trying to process—he expected these few weeks of substituting for his father in Cannon Beach to be a walk in the park.

Chapter Two

"You're late." Carmen Marquez, the clinic's receptionist and office manager, gave an arch look over the top of her readers, and Melissa winced but held up her braced wrist.

"I know. It's been a crazy day. I'm sorry. Blame it on this."

"What did you do? Punch somebody?" Tiffany Lowell, one of their certified nursing assistants, gave her a wide-eyed look—though the college student and part-time band front woman wore so much makeup, she had the same expression most of the time.

"I tripped over a big, goofy Irish setter and sprained my wrist. I'm sorry I'm late, but I was on strict orders to rest and put ice on it."

"That's exactly what you should be doing. In fact,

it's what Dr. Sanderson would be telling you to do if he were here," Carmen said.

Dr. Sanderson Jr. *had* been the one to give her the instructions, but she wasn't ready to share that interesting bit of gossip with the other women.

"You look like you're either going to puke or pass out," Tiffany observed.

"We don't have any patients scheduled for another half hour," Carmen said with a great deal more sympathy in her voice. "You should at least sit down."

"I'm fine. I need to get ready for the new doctor. He should be coming in today."

Carmen angled her head in a strange way, her mouth pursed and her eyes twinkling. "He's already here. Oh, honey. Have we got a surprise for you."

The butterflies that had been dancing in her stomach since earlier on the beach seemed to pick up their pace. "The substitute doctor is Dr. Sanderson's son, Eli."

"Whoa! Did your fall make you psychic or something?" Tiffany asked with much more respect than she usually awarded Melissa.

"In a way, I guess you could say that. Sort of. I bumped into him on the beach this morning. He was a firsthand witness when I made my graceful face-plant into the sand, and he ended up kindly helping me up."

The memory of the concern in his blue eyes and of his strong fingers holding her hand, his skin warm against hers, made her nerve endings tingle.

She firmly clamped down on the memory. She would have to work closely with him for at least the next few weeks while Wendell recovered. It would be a disaster if she couldn't manage to keep a lid on her unexpected attraction to the man.

"I keep forgetting you grew up in town," Carmen said. "You must know Eli, then."

While Cannon Beach could swarm with tourists during the summer months, it was really a small town at heart. Most permanent residents knew one another.

"We went to school together. He was older. I was a freshman the year he was a senior. I didn't know he was going to be filling in until I bumped into him this morning. Last I heard, we were getting a temp from the Portland agency."

"That's what I heard, too," Carmen said. "I guess we have to roll with what we get."

"I'm pretty sure plenty of women in Cannon Beach will want to roll with Doc Sanderson's son when they see him." Tiffany smirked.

Melissa turned her shocked laugh into a cough. "He told me he wasn't sure until the last minute whether he'd be able to make it back to fill in."

"You know where he's been, right?" Carmen asked.

"Some kind of war zone," Tiffany said.

Wendell had told her something about what his son was doing, how since finishing his internship in emergency medicine several years earlier, Eli had been on a special assignment from the military to work with aid agencies, setting up medical clinics and providing care to desperate, helpless people whose countries were in turmoil. He had been deployed almost constantly over the last five years.

Wendell had been so proud of his son for stepping

up, even though his service put him in harm's way time and again. He had also been worried for him.

"He feels things so deeply," her boss had said. "I can't imagine it's easy, the kinds of things he has to see now."

She remembered feeling great sympathy for Eli and admiration for him, though at the time she had pictured him as the nerdy, scholarly, skinny teenager she remembered, not the buff, gorgeous man she had encountered that morning on the beach.

"One thing I need to ask, though. Maybe you know the answer," Carmen said. "How can he just show up in Cannon Beach and start practicing medicine here? Do I need to check with the licensing board? Doesn't he need an Oregon license or something?"

"Fun and interesting fact. The particular license given to U.S. Army doctors allows them to practice medicine anywhere."

Melissa could feel her vertebrae stiffen and nerves flutter at the deep voice from behind her.

Oh, it was going to be a long two or three weeks if she didn't take control of this ridiculous crush she had suddenly formed for Eli Sanderson.

"I guess that makes sense," Carmen said.

"Yes," he answered. "Think how confusing it would be if an army doc had to go before the licensing board every time he was called to an emergency or had a new assignment."

"That would be a serious pain." Melissa hated the slightly breathless note in her voice. She sounded ridiculous, like the kind of brainless bikini-clad groupies who used to follow the pro surfers on the circuit.

She cleared her throat, wishing she could clear away her nerves as easily.

"Good to know. I'll file that little tidbit away, in case I'm ever on a game show where 'Army Doctors' is a category."

Tiffany snorted, and Eli's mouth quirked up into a little smile, teeth flashing. She had the strangest feeling he hadn't found that many things to smile about lately, though she couldn't have said exactly why she had that impression.

"That would be the most boring game show ever," he said. "Unless you love learning about regulations and protocol."

"I really don't. As long as you can legally see your father's patients, that's all I care about."

"I'll do my best. I know he's been worried about his caseload."

"Your dad is a great doctor, but he worries too much about his patients," Tiffany said.

"Is that possible?" Eli asked.

"He should have worried a little more about himself. He could barely stand up the last few weeks before the surgery."

Tiffany was a bit rough around the edges but like everyone else, she adored Dr. Sanderson and frequently told patients how cool it was that she now worked for the doctor who had delivered her twenty years earlier.

"Your father was so worried about taking time away from his patients he almost didn't have the surgery, though his specialist has been urging him to for months. At least as long as I've been here," Melissa said.

"Longer," Carmen said, her expression exasperated. The older woman liked to mother everyone, even their boss, who was at least two or three years older than the office manager.

"I think he would have continued putting it off and hobbling around if he hadn't injured the right one so badly two weeks ago," Melissa said. "Then the surgery became not only urgent but imperative."

"Everything worked out for the best," Eli said. "I was able to create a gap in my schedule and here I am, at least for a few weeks."

Yes. Here you are.

She had thought him gorgeous in skintight workout clothes. That was nothing compared to the sight of him in khaki slacks, a white exam coat and a crisply ironed button-down shirt a few shades lighter than his blue eyes.

She had been a nurse for years and had never been particularly drawn to a physician, until right this moment.

"How's the wrist?" he asked.

At his words, the pain she had been staving off seemed to rush back. She held up the brace and wriggled her fingers. "Still aches but it's bearable. I agree with you that I should hold off a day or two before I have it x-rayed."

"Did you have any time to put ice on it?"

"A few minutes. Which is the main reason I'm late."

"Good. That's the best thing you can do."

They lapsed into silence and she tried to keep from gawking at him. She loved her job, working with Wendell Sanderson. The man had been nothing but kind to her since the day she'd come back to Cannon Beach. She hated thinking things would be awkward and uncomfortable with Eli here.

She could handle anything for a few weeks, Melissa reminded herself. Even working for a man for whom she had developed a serious thirst.

"Can you give me the charts of those who have appointments today? I'd like to try familiarizing myself with their files."

His words were directed to Carmen yet still provided Melissa the reminder she needed. He was her boss and she couldn't forget that.

"I've already pulled the charts of those coming in this morning. They're on your dad's desk, since I figured you would be setting up in there," the office manager replied. "I'll find the rest and bring them in for you."

"Thank you." He gave the woman a polite smile, and Melissa could swear she felt her ovaries melt.

When he walked back down the hallway toward his office, Melissa slumped into one of the chairs in the waiting room.

Oh, this was not good. At all. She might have silently wished for a man this morning, but in truth she didn't have time for that kind of complication. She had Skye and work and friends, not to mention the online classes she was taking to work toward her nurse practitioner license. There was no room left for her to be stupid about Eli.

"Are you okay?" Carmen asked.

"I will be."

Eventually.

"He seems nice, doesn't he?" Tiffany said. "Dr. Sanderson talks about his son like all the time, but I always pictured him different, somehow. Since he's in the army, I thought he'd have a buzz cut and be all harsh and by the book."

She hadn't pictured him at all, hadn't really given Eli Sanderson much thought over the years. Now she was afraid she would be able to think about little else.

Even her throbbing wrist couldn't seem to distract her.

"How did your first day go? Any problems or unique diagnoses you think I need to know about?"

Eli adjusted his dad's pillow, giving him a stern look. "Your only job right now is to focus on healing from this surgery. I can take care of your patients, got it? You don't need to worry about them."

"I have no concerns on that front," Wendell assured him. "You're a better doctor than I ever could have dreamed of being at your age."

Eli knew that was far from true. How could it be? His own dreams were haunted by the ghosts of all those he couldn't save. Miri. Justine. Those ghosts at least had names and faces, but there were scores of others who drifted through, anonymous and lost.

He let out a breath, wondering when the hell the sense of guilt and loss would leave him. It had been six months but still felt like yesterday.

He turned his attention back to his father, instead of that war-battered market town.

"Dad, I could never be half the doctor you are. We both know that. I'll be trying my whole life to catch up."

His father rolled his eyes. "We could be here all day patting each other on the back, but I know what I know.

And what I know is that you're a damn fine doctor and I'm proud to call you my son. There's no one else on earth I would trust more than you to fill in for me while I'm laid up. When I ask about my patients, it's only because I'm concerned about them, not because I don't think you can care for them the way I would."

His father had been the best doctor Eli knew. Wendell and his genuine concern for his patients had been the main reason Eli had gone to medical school in the first place. He had wanted to help people, to deliver babies and diagnose illnesses and give little kids their first shots.

He had never expected that his first years of practicing medicine would be in a series of emergency shelters and refugee camps, but that was the path he had chosen and he couldn't regret it.

"If I'm not mistaken, that sweet Julia Garrett was supposed to come in today for a prenatal checkup. She and Will had an early-term miscarriage during her last pregnancy, so I've been watching her closely. How did things look today?"

Though he instinctively wanted to tell his father to put all his patients out of his head, Eli knew that wouldn't happen. Wendell wanted to stay current on all the people he had cared for over thirty-five years of practicing in Cannon Beach. Eli had a feeling that was the only way his father would be able to endure the long recovery from his double knee replacement.

"Everything looked good today. The baby measured exactly where she should be at this stage in the pregnancy, the heartbeat sounded strong and steady, and Julia appears healthy and happy. She didn't report any unusual concerns."

"Oh, that's good. This is her fourth pregnancy—fifth, if you count the baby they lost and sixth if you count the fact that her first were twins—and I wanted her to feel confident and comfortable."

As far as Eli was concerned, his father was the iconic family physician. Wendell was dedicated to his patients, compassionate over their troubles and driven to provide them the best possible care. He had delivered some of his own patients—like Will Garrett—and was now delivering the second generation and providing care over their children.

Those patients had saved his father, plucking him out of the deep depression Wendell had fallen into after Eli's mother died following a short but hard-fought battle against breast cancer when Eli was twelve.

They had both been devastated and had dealt with the blow in different ways. Eli had retreated into books, withdrawing from his friends, from baseball, from social activities. His father had done the same, focusing only on his patients and on his son.

The pain of losing Ada Sanderson had eased over the years but hadn't left completely. Eli suspected it never would.

"And how are you, son? I mean, how are you *really*? You haven't talked about what happened with that friend of yours, but I know it still eats at you."

The question, so intuitive, seemed to knock his own knees out from under him. It had always seemed impossible to conceal his inner struggles from his father's gimlet gaze. Still, Eli did his best. He had never told Wendell how close he had been to Justine, or how her death and Miri's had been his fault.

Somehow he managed to summon an expression he hoped resembled a smile. "I'm good. Why wouldn't I be? It's a beautiful time of year to be home in Oregon. I don't remember the last April I was here. I'm not sure what I'm looking forward to more—watching the spring storms churning across the water or savoring the explosion of flowers."

Wendell saw right through him, as usual. His father gave him a searching look even as he shifted on his hospital bed to find a more comfortable position.

"After all the exotic places the army has sent you, are you sure you won't be bored out of your mind treating cold sores and high blood pressure?"

"No. I'm looking forward to that, too, if you want the truth. It will be a nice, calm change of pace. Just what I need to decompress."

"Maybe this will help you figure out whether you're going to stay in the military or settle down somewhere and open a practice. Or maybe join a practice that's already busy with tourists and locals alike."

Since the day Eli finished his residency, Wendell had been after him to become his partner here.

It had always been in his long-range plan, but how could he walk away now, with this heavy sense of responsibility he carried everywhere? He felt the weight of it even more on his shoulders now, after what happened to Justine. She had been dedicated, compassionate, completely driven to help those in turmoil. Her dedication had been silenced forever and she could no longer carry out her work. He had made a vow to carry on in her place.

"Tell me how they have been treating you here," he said to change the subject. "Have you already charmed all the nurses?"

"Not all of them. A few of these nurses have been coming to my office since they were children. I'm afraid they know all my tricks by now."

Wendell was regaling him with a story about the surgeon who had operated on him when Eli heard a slight knock on the door.

A moment later, it was pushed open, and a delicate-looking girl of about seven held the door open while cradling a huge cellophane-wrapped basket in the other.

"Hi, Dr. Sanderson," she said cheerfully, giving his father a winsome smile.

Wendell beamed back at her. "Well, hello there, my dear. Isn't this a lovely surprise?"

She gave a grin, missing her two front teeth, and held up the basket. "This is for you. My mom was busy talking to her friend at the nurses station and I got tired of waiting for her, so I told her I would come by myself. This thing is *heavy*."

"Eli, help my friend Skye out and take that big basket from her before her arms break right off, will you?"

He dutifully rose so he could take the basket out of the girl's arms and set it on the small table next to his father's bed.

While he was occupied, the girl stole his chair, the one right next to Wendell's bedside.

"That stuff is all for you" she said, pointing to the

basket. "Even the candy. My mom and I went shopping in three different stores, trying to find all the things you love."

"That is so sweet of you. Your mother is a treasure and so are you, my dear."

She giggled. "My grandma says I'm a pill and too big for my britches."

"I don't doubt that's true," Wendell said.

The girl turned to Eli with a curious look. "Hi," she said brightly. "I'm Skye Fielding. What's your name?"

When she identified herself, he gave her a closer look. Skye Fielding. This had to be Melissa's daughter. He should have picked up the resemblance before she even identified herself. Now he could see she shared the same vivid green eyes with her mother and the same dimple that appeared and disappeared on one side of her mouth.

"This is my son, Elias Alexander Sanderson."

"Whoa. That's a big name. It's..." She counted on her small fingers. "Ten syllables."

Yes. He was fully aware. Try filling out all those letters on military forms designed for guys named Joe Smith. "You can call me Eli," he said.

"Hi, Eli." She settled deeper into his chair, perfectly at home, which he found more amusing than anything he'd seen in a long time. With nowhere else to sit in the room, he leaned against the sink.

"Mom says you got brand-new knees because your old ones hurt you all the time," she said.

"*Old* is the key word there," Wendell muttered.

His father wasn't that old. He was only in his early sixties and vibrant for his age. Why hadn't Wendell started dating and married someone? His father was still a handsome man. Judging by all the flowers and cards in his room, he was fairly popular around town, too. Maybe Eli could work on that while he was home.

"My mom says you have to stay here for two whole weeks!"

She seemed positively aghast at the idea.

"It's not that bad. They have fun things to do all day long. Games and movies and music time. Plus, they serve good food and have free popcorn in the cafeteria."

Eli had a feeling Wendell was trying to convince himself as much as he was the little girl. His father wasn't thrilled about the time that loomed ahead of him in the rehabilitation center, but that was the price for his impatience and desire to do both knees at the same time, when he needed daily therapy and his house wasn't fully accessible.

"Free popcorn! You're lucky. I love popcorn."

"So do I, but if I eat all the free popcorn, I might have a tough time getting back on my feet."

"I guess." She appeared to consider that. "Do you think I could have some now?"

Wendell laughed. "Maybe. You'll have to ask your mom. Where do you think she is?"

"Probably still talking to her friend," Skye said.

A moment later, as if to prove her daughter wrong, Melissa appeared in the doorway, looking slightly frazzled.

He had seen her three times that day, in three different wardrobe changes.

This morning on the beach, she had been wearing running clothes—leggings and a comfortable-looking hoodie, with her hair up in a ponytail. All day he had been aware of her moving around the office in burgundy-colored scrubs and a black cardigan. Tonight, Melissa had changed into jeans and a soft coral sweater and had let her hair down to curl around her shoulders.

He wasn't sure which version he found more attractive. It was a little like being asked to choose among his favorite ice cream flavors.

"Oh," she exclaimed, slightly breathless, with a stern look to her daughter. "Here you are. I didn't know where you went. I was busy talking to Jan and when I turned around, you had completely disappeared."

He could still see the shadows of unease in her expression and felt a wave of sympathy. He didn't have children, but he knew that panicked feeling of not being able to find someone you cared for deeply. He had a flashback of running through a panicked crowd, everyone else screaming and trying to escape the market center while he ran toward the chaos and fear. He closed his eyes, trying to scrub it away and return to the moment.

"I told you two times I was going to carry the basket to room forty-one," Skye informed her mother. "I guess you just didn't hear me."

More of Melissa's fear seemed to seep away and she hugged her child. "I'm sorry, honey. Jan is an old friend of mine from nursing school. I didn't know she was working here. I'm afraid I got a little distracted, catching up with her."

"My arms were too tired to keep holding the basket, so I found the room and gave it myself to Dr. Sanderson."

"I see that. Thanks, kiddo." She ran a hand over her

daughter's hair and the sweet, tender familiarity of the gesture sent an odd lump rising in his throat.

The unexpected emotions intensified when she leaned forward and kissed Wendell on the cheek.

"And how are you? How are the new knees?"

His father shrugged, clearly pleased at the visit from Melissa and her daughter. "I can't complain. Though I'm not ready to dance the salsa yet, I can tell they're already less painful than the old ones. They'll be even better once I break them in."

"Don't be in too big of a rush. How many times have I heard you tell your patients that true healing takes time?"

His father made a face. "Do you know how annoying it is to have your own words thrown back in your face?"

She laughed. "It's for your own good."

"I know." He gestured to the brace she wore. "What happened to your wrist?"

Her gaze shifted to Eli, and he thought he saw a soft brush of color soak her cheeks. "It's a long story. Let's just say Fiona was in a strange mood this morning and I fell. But it's feeling much better. Your son checked it out for me."

Whether she had wanted him to or not. She didn't say the words, but he had a feeling she was thinking them.

"That's good to hear. He's a good boy and an excellent doctor. I've been waiting for him to come back so he can meet you."

Oh, no. That sounded entirely too much like matchmaking. He had to cut that off before Wendell got any inappropriate ideas.

"We've met, Dad. You remember. Melissa and I went

to high school together for a year, though I'm older. I knew her ex-husband, too."

"My dad got married again and his wife is going to have a baby."

Melissa gave her daughter an exasperated look, and Eli had the feeling she wasn't thrilled with Skye for sharing that particular nugget of information.

"Yes," she said. "We're very happy for them both."

"Sounds like you've got a lot on your plate," Wendell said. "That makes your visit mean even more. A visit would have been enough, you know. You didn't have to bring along a huge care package, so heavy your strong seven-year-old daughter could barely carry it."

"It's only a few things, I promise. The fancy packaging always makes baskets look bigger than they are."

Except for that fleeting glance, she seemed to be avoiding looking at him directly. Why? Had he done something wrong that day in the office? There had been a little awkwardness early on, but Eli had thought by the end of the day they had started to establish a bit of a comfortable rhythm.

Skye nudged the basket closer to Wendell. "Open it. I want to see if you like the stuff we picked out."

"I'm sure I will love everything. It came from you, so of course I will." He smiled at the girl, who beamed back at him.

His father's rapport with both Melissa and her daughter didn't surprise him. Wendell loved people, one reason his staff adored him and his patients returned to him for generations.

"Go on," Skye pressed. "Open it."

He helped his father out by setting the basket on Wendell's lap, then watched as his father went through the contents. There was nothing elaborate, but all the gifts seemed thoughtful and sweet—a paperback mystery he knew Wendell would adore, a book of crossword puzzles, a box of chocolates and a bag of lemon drops, a journal, a soft-looking knit throw that would feel perfect on chilly spring mornings.

His father was delighted with all of it.

"Thank you so very much," he said after he had unearthed each new delight. "How did I ever get so lucky to have you both in my life?"

"We're the lucky ones," Melissa said with a smile.

"I don't have a grandpa and he doesn't have a grandkid, so Dr. Wendell said we can both pretend we belong to each other," Skye informed Eli.

It warmed his heart that Melissa appeared to watch out for his father. She struck him as someone who couldn't help caring about others. He had witnessed it all day. Even with her own injured wrist, she had been kind and caring to each patient they had seen.

"What are you two up to tonight, besides coming here and making my day?" Wendell asked them.

"We're going to have pizza," Skye informed him. "It's Friday and we always have pizza on Friday. Sometimes we make it ourselves and sometimes we order it from a pizza place and sometimes we go out. Tonight we're going out."

"Nice. Where are you heading?"

"We're going to A Slice of Heaven."

"Oh, good choice," Wendell said. "It's one of my favorites. Have you been there yet, son?"

Considering Eli had only been back in town for thirty-six hours and had been working or sleeping for most of that time—or visiting his father—hitting all the local hot spots hadn't exactly been on his priority list. "Not yet."

"You can't miss it. Trust me," his father said.

"You could come with us," Skye offered with that charmer of a smile. "Mom says maybe we can even get cheesy bread. They have the *best* cheesy bread."

"It's been a long day," Melissa said, a trace of defiance in her voice. "I need a few carbs to the rescue."

He wanted to suggest she also might need to rest and ice her wrist, but he didn't want to stand in the way of a girl and her carbs.

His father shifted on the bed and yawned, his mouth drawn and his eyes clouding with exhaustion.

"We should go," Melissa said, picking up the hint. "Come on, Skye."

"Do you have to?" Wendell said, though Eli heard the exhaustion in his voice.

"I should go, too, so you can get some rest. That's the best thing for you, in case your doctor hasn't mentioned it."

"He has," Wendell said glumly. "I hate being in this hospital bed."

"You know what they say about doctors making the worst patients. Try to behave yourself. I'll stop by tomorrow."

"Thanks."

His father rolled over, and Eli could tell he was already dozing off. He followed Melissa and her daughter out of the room.

"That was thoughtful of you, bringing a care package to my father," he said when they were out in the hallway. "It obviously touched him."

"Dr. Sanderson has been nothing but kind to us since we moved back to town. It's the very least we can do, giving him a few things to help him pass the time while he's laid up. He's a wonderful man, your father."

"He is."

"Seriously. I've worked with a lot of jerk doctors in my day and your father is a breath of fresh air, as compassionate to his staff as he is to his patients."

"It's always good to hear my own opinion confirmed by those who work closely with him."

"Not gonna lie. He's my favorite of all the doctors I've ever worked with. You have big shoes to fill."

"My feet will never fit in those shoes. Why do you think I haven't come home before now to try? I just have to do my best to stumble along as best I can while I'm here."

That was probably more revealing than he intended, at least judging by the probing look Melissa sent his way. He opted to change the subject. "So you're off to have pizza?"

"Yep. Like I said, we always have pizza on Friday night," Skye told him. "Pizza on Friday, Tacos on Tuesday. The rest of the time, we like to mix things up."

He found it charming that she included herself in the meal-planning process. As precocious as the girl seemed, he wouldn't be surprised if she could fix a gourmet meal all by herself, given the chance.

"That's good. You wouldn't want to be too predictable."

"What are you having for dinner?" Skye asked him.

"I don't know. I haven't crossed that bridge yet. Unfortunately, I do *not* have a pizza-on-Friday tradition, but it sounds good."

More than likely, he would head back to his father's house and make a sandwich or heat up a TV dinner—neither of which sounded very appetizing compared to the carbtastic wonders of A Slice of Heaven.

"You could come with us," Skye suggested.

He glanced at Melissa, who looked taken aback by the invitation. She didn't seem crazy about the idea, yet Eli was surprised at how very much he wanted to accept. The idea of eating alone again at his father's house held no appeal.

"I don't want to impose on your night out together."

"We eat together every night," Skye said. "Besides, pizza always tastes better when it's shared. It's a scientific fact. Anyway, that's what my mom says."

"Funny. I don't remember learning about that in school."

He sent a sidelong look to Melissa, who shrugged and blushed at the same time.

"You must have missed the breakthrough study. Plus, when you share a pizza, the calories don't count."

"Good to know. I wasn't aware."

"But you've probably had a long day," she said. "Don't let us pressure you into it."

He should gracefully back out of it. She didn't want

him there anyway. But he found he wasn't willing to do it. He wanted pizza and he wanted to spend more time with her. Neither craving was necessarily good for him, but that didn't seem to matter.

"I haven't had pizza from A Slice of Heaven in years. Now that you've planted that seed, I'm afraid nothing else will do except that. Thank you for inviting me."

She paused, then gave a smile that seemed only a little forced. "Great. Do you remember where the pizza parlor is?"

"I could probably find it in my sleep. I'll meet you there."

"See you." Skye tugged on her mom's hand. "Let's go. I'm starving!"

She followed her daughter out of the rehab center, and he watched them go for a moment before following closely behind.

As delicious as the wood-fired pizza was at the beloved seaside pizzeria, he found Melissa and her daughter even more appealing.

Chapter Three

In her long and illustrious history of bad ideas, inviting Dr. Eli Sanderson out to grab pizza with them had to rank right up there with the lousy perm she got in seventh grade and losing her virginity to Cody Fielding after the prom her junior year.

Technically, Skye had invited Eli, but Melissa should have figured out a polite way to wiggle out of it, for all of their sakes.

Why *had* Skye invited him along? Her daughter did love Dr. Sanderson Sr., but she usually wasn't so spontaneously open to strangers.

Maybe her daughter had responded, as Melissa did, to that air of loneliness about Eli. She couldn't put her finger on it, but there was just something *sad* about him. A shadow in his eye, a particular set to his mouth.

She had tried hard to teach Skye how important it was to be kind to others. Okay, maybe she tried to overcompensate a little on her end, knowing her daughter wouldn't receive similar lessons on the rare occasions she was with her dad. Maybe she had tried *too* hard, if Skye was going to go around inviting random gorgeous men to share their Friday-night tradition.

So much for her lectures all day about keeping her head on straight around him. That was fine advice in a professional setting when he was her boss but might be harder to remember in social situations.

It was no big deal. They were only sharing pizza. A Slice of Heaven had notoriously fast service, even on the weekend. With any luck, they could be seated, served and out of there within an hour. Surely she could manage to control her hormones for sixty lousy minutes.

"I like the second Dr. Sanderson," Skye said from the back seat as they drove to the restaurant. "He seems nice...maybe not quite as nice as the first Dr. Sanderson, but better than Dr. Wu or Dr. Charles. Whenever they used to talk to me, they never even looked at me. It's like they didn't think a kid could have anything important to say."

How did a seven-year-old girl become so very perceptive? The doctors in the clinic where Melissa worked in Honolulu before coming back to Cannon Beach had treated *her* that way, too, as if her opinions didn't matter.

"They were very good doctors," she said.

"But are they nice humans?"

That was an excellent question. She hadn't been sorry to leave, though her coworkers had only been one of the reasons she had moved from Honolulu back to Oregon. Her mother was here, for one thing, and she found she missed being close to Sharon.

And the cost of living had been prohibitive. She had stayed in Hawaii for the last few years mostly because Cody had lived there and she wanted to do all she could to keep Skye's father in her daughter's life. His visitations had become so few and far between as he traveled around on the professional surfer circuit that her efforts had begun to seem laughable. When he had told her the previous summer he was moving again, she had given up trying.

Skye needed a stable home base. Melissa couldn't keep dragging her from town to town, hoping Cody would eventually start paying attention to their child. She had tried for years after the divorce, then decided being closer to her own mother would provide more benefit to her child than infrequent, disappointing visits with her immature father.

Melissa would have loved four or five children, but life hadn't worked out the way she planned. Good thing the one daughter she had was so amazing. Skye was smart and kind and amazingly intuitive for a child.

"Can I play pool tonight at A Slice of Heaven?"

And persistent. Once an idea took root in her head, she could never let it go.

"If there's an empty table, maybe. Otherwise, nope," Melissa said as she pulled into the pizzeria's restaurant, the same answer she gave every time they came.

The people who hung out at the popular restaurant and played at the three tables in the back were serious about the game. They were probably good humans, but they weren't at all patient with a seven-year-old girl just learning how to wield a cue.

Skye sighed as they parked and walked toward the restaurant but she didn't argue, to Melissa's relief. Her wrist was throbbing, and she really wanted to go home and rest it. She would definitely break out the ice pack after her daughter was in bed.

A wave of garlic and the delicious scent of the pizzeria's wood-fired crusts hit the moment Melissa opened the door. Oh, yeah, she suddenly remembered. She was starving. She'd kind of forgotten that while she was talking to Wendell and Eli. Now her stomach growled and she had a fleeting wish that the wisecrack she had made to Eli was true, that none of the calories or carbs of the delicious Slice of Heaven pies counted when they were shared.

Somehow Eli had made it there before they did. He was inside talking to the hostess and daughter of the owner, Gina Salvaticci, who had been a year or two ahead of Melissa. She had never liked her much, she remembered now. Gina had been friends with Cody before Melissa and her family moved to Cannon Beach, and always acted as if she thought Melissa wasn't good enough for him. Since the divorce and Melissa's return to town, she hadn't necessarily warmed to her.

If her father's restaurant didn't serve such good pizza, Melissa would do whatever she could to avoid her. Fortunately, Gina usually wasn't here on Fridays.

But she was here *this Friday, and* Gina looked as shocked by the changes in quiet, nerdy Eli Sanderson as Melissa had been and she was obviously flirting with him. She touched his arm as she spoke to him and looked at him from under her half-closed lids, her body facing him and her mouth slightly open.

Melissa felt a sharp kick in her gut, a weird tension, and realized with chagrin that she was jealous of the other woman, even though Eli seemed completely oblivious to any interested body language.

He looked up when they approached. "Here's the rest of my party. You said you had a table ready for us?"

Gina turned and Melissa knew the moment she spotted her. Her gaze narrowed and her hand slid away from Eli. Gina didn't look at all pleased to see another woman joining him.

Melissa couldn't really blame her. A hot doctor coming back to town, even temporarily, was bound to stir up all the single women.

Not *her.* She was willing to entertain a friendship with the man but that was all she could give him. She had no room in her life for anything more, especially not a wandering doctor who would be heading off to the next hot spot on the globe the moment his dad had his knees under him again. Been there, done that, with a man whose career was far more important than his family. She would never even consider it again.

Her priority had to be Skye, and providing her daughter the most stable home life possible, after the chaos of her daughter's earlier years.

She smiled to let the other woman know she wasn't a threat. If Gina was interested in Eli, she should go for it.

"Right this way," Gina said coolly.

She led them back to a fairly good table with a nice view of the sunset.

"Will this be okay for you?" Gina asked. She looked only at Eli when she asked the question. He in turn deferred to Melissa.

"Does this work for you and Skye?" he asked.

"Looks great," she answered. "Thanks."

He reached for the back of a chair and pulled it back. Nobody had held a chair out for her in such a long time, it took Melissa an awkward moment to realize he meant for her to sit there.

"Uh. Thanks."

She *really* needed to get out more.

She sat down and Skye plopped into the seat next to her.

"Can I get a root beer?" she asked.

They had a pretty strict no-soda/low-sugar rule 95 percent of the time, but Melissa tended to relax a bit on pizza night. "One. A small."

"I'll let your server know," Gina said. "Here's a couple of menus," Gina said. "Our special tonight is the arugula and prosciutto with our house-pulled mozzarella."

"Sounds delicious," Eli said. "Thanks."

The next few minutes were spent perusing the menu. Skye ordered her favorite, half cheese, half pepperoni, while Melissa and Eli both ordered the special, along with salads with the house dressing on the side and, of course, an order of their cheesy bread.

"If I can't play pool, can I at least go play the pinball machine?" Skye asked. "I brought all my own quarters."

"All of them? I thought you were saving up for a new scooter like your friend Alice has."

"I am. But Sonia gave me two dollars for helping her pull weeds yesterday, so I put that in my piggy bank and took out six quarters."

Skye reached into her pocket and pulled out change that jingled as she set it on the table. "I want to see if I can do better than last time we came."

"It's your money. If that's the way you want to spend it, go for it."

"Thanks."

She shoved her chair back and hurried to the row of gaming machines along one wall of the pizzeria. This was an ideal setup, where she could keep an eye on her daughter but didn't have to stand right over her shoulder.

"She seems like a sweet kid," Eli said. "I know my dad thinks so, anyway."

Melissa had made plenty of mistakes in her life—including a disastrous marriage—but her daughter was not among them.

"She's amazing. Kind, compassionate, funny. I won the kid lottery."

He smiled at that and sipped at the beer their server had brought him. "Does she see her father very often?"

All her frustrations from earlier in the day rushed back, and Melissa did her best not to tense.

"Not as often as she'd like. It's been tough to have a relationship when he's always heading to the next beach with the pro surf circuit."

"Must have made it tough on a marriage."

"You could say that."

"How long have you and Cody been divorced?"

"We split up when Skye was three and officially divorced a year later."

"And she's, what, seven now?"

"Yes."

The sense of failure never quite left Melissa, even after four years. She knew she had no reason to feel guilty, but somehow she couldn't seem to help it.

She didn't tell Eli how hard she had tried to salvage the marriage for her child or how even after it became clear that Cody wouldn't stop cheating, she had chosen to stay in Hawaii, Cody's surfing home base, so her daughter could still see her father.

"Where is he these days?"

"He's coming back to Oregon. His new wife is expecting a baby, and he wants to be closer to his family in Portland so they can help her out."

She wouldn't let herself be bitter about that. When *Melissa* had been pregnant with Skye, Cody hadn't been nearly as solicitous about her needs. He'd been training for a big wave competition, totally focused on it, and couldn't take time away. Instead, they had lived in a crappy studio apartment on the North Shore. He had refused to come back to Oregon, even for her to deliver the baby close to her mom.

Maybe the fact that he was putting his new wife and unborn baby first for once was proof that her ex was finally growing up. She hoped so, but she didn't think anyone could blame her for being skeptical.

"And how long have you been back in Cannon Beach?"

"About seven months. For the past few years, Cody's home base has been Oahu. Last year he moved overseas, so I decided it was time Skye and I came back to be closer to family."

"That's nice. And you live in Brambleberry House."

"For now. We love it there, but I'm saving up to buy a house."

"And going to school, I understand. Carmen or Tiffany mentioned it today."

"I'm working to become a family nurse practitioner," she said as their server set down salads in front of the two of them.

"How's that going?"

"Not going to lie, it's been tough while juggling a full-time job and a child. I still have two years to go. I can do most of the work online, which helps."

"That's terrific. There's such a need for well-trained nurse practitioners right now. Good for you."

The approving look in his eyes sent warmth seeping through her. Going to school and working was tough work, and she had sacrificed sleep and a social life for it, but she was trying to build a solid future for her and her child. All the sacrifices were worthwhile, an investment toward security for Skye.

"What about you? I'm surprised you haven't done the whole family thing yet."

He shrugged, a hint of a shadow in his eyes. "You know how it is. Some guys can handle starting a family while they're in med school, but I wasn't one of them."

"You've been out of med school—what?—five or six years now? There hasn't been a chance in all those years to find somebody you want to make Mrs. Dr. Elias Sanderson?"

"No," he said quickly. Too quickly. The shadows seemed to intensify. Eli Sanderson had secrets. What were they? She had the feeling he had lost someone close to him. Was it a woman?

She wanted to probe, but Skye came back before she could ask a follow-up question.

She was relieved, she told herself. Eli's secrets were none of her business. He was her employer, at least for the next few weeks. Okay, he might also be becoming a friend. That didn't mean she needed to know everything that had happened to him since the day he had left Cannon Beach for college.

"Your quarters are gone already?" she asked her daughter.

"Pinball is *hard*," Skye complained. "Simon made it look so easy."

Simon was the son of her friends Will and Julia Garrett, twin to Maddie, a girl who sometimes babysat Skye for her. The last time they had come to A Slice of Heaven, their family had been there, too, and Skye had been fascinated, watching the older boy.

"Simon is a teenager, honey. Almost eighteen. He's probably had a lot of practice at it."

She pouted but didn't have time to fret more as their server fortuitously came by just then with their pizzas, fragrant and hot.

They were all too busy the next few moments savoring their meal, which didn't leave a lot of room for talking.

In between bites, Skye kept looking back toward the billiards tables with a wistful look.

"You look like you're wanting to try your hand at pool," Eli said.

"Mom says I can't. It's too busy here on Friday nights. There are people waiting their turn to play."

"My dad has a billiards table in the sunroom," Eli said. "You're welcome to come over and practice a little there before you try to play in the big leagues over here at A Slice of Heaven."

"Thanks," Skye said, eyes wide with excitement.

Melissa tried to hide her frown. She really wished he hadn't said that. Eli would forget he made the offer, but Skye wouldn't.

Her daughter had spent entirely too much time being disappointed by empty promises. She didn't need more.

Maybe she was being too cynical. Maybe he wouldn't forget.

She distracted Skye with their favorite game of I Spy for the rest of the meal, and Eli joined in willingly. He had a unique eye and stumped both her and Skye more than once with the things he observed.

"I'm totally stuffed now," Skye said after two slices. She eased back in her chair and placed her hands over her belly.

Eli chuckled. "That was delicious, wasn't it? The best pizza I've had in a long time. I forgot how delicious the crust here is."

"They have a magic recipe," Melissa said.

"They must, especially if they can make it calorie-free."

His smile made her hormones sigh. Seriously, this was becoming ridiculous.

After they boxed up their leftover pizza, Eli insisted on paying the tab. She would have argued, but her friend Sage and her husband, Eben, part owners of Brambleberry House, came in at that moment and distracted her. By the time she waved goodbye to her friends, the server had already completed the bill.

"Next time is my treat," she said.

"I'll look forward to it," he answered. His words had a ring of sincerity that again warmed her far more than they should.

They walked outside into a lovely April night, rich with the scent of the ocean, with flowers, with new life.

She could hear the low murmur of the waves along with the constant coastal wind that rustled the new leaves of the trees next to the restaurant.

Oh, she had missed it here. She had lived in many beautiful, exotic places since she'd left Cannon Beach, but none of them had been the same. She had lived here longer than anywhere, from the age of thirteen to eighteen. It was home to her.

"That was lovely," he said when they reached their respective vehicles in the parking lot. "The most enjoyable meal I've had in a long time. Thank you for inviting me."

"You're welcome. Thank you for insisting on paying for it."

"Yeah. Thanks," Skye said cheerfully. "It was fun."

Melissa couldn't make a habit of it. She was far too drawn to him.

"Have a good evening, Eli."

Their gazes met, and those shadows prompted her to do something completely uncharacteristic. She stood on tiptoe and kissed his cheek, intending it only as a warm, friendly, welcome-home kind of gesture.

He smelled delicious, of soap and male skin, and it was all she could do not to stand there and inhale.

She forced herself to ease away, regretting the impulse with every passing moment.

"Good night, Melissa. Skye, it was a pleasure. Persuade your mom to take you to my dad's place sometime soon so you can practice your pool game."

"I will! Thanks."

"See you Monday," she said.

"Put some ice on that wrist," he answered, his voice gruff.

She nodded and ushered her daughter to her vehicle. Though her wrist still ached, the injury seemed a lifetime ago.

Chapter Four

Melissa managed to make it through the rest of the weekend without obsessing too much about Eli, mainly because she and Skye spent Saturday running errands, then drove to Portland for the day on Sunday. By Sunday night, the prospect of going back to the clinic and spending the day in his company filled her with nerves.

She managed to push it away by baking strawberry shortcake Sunday evening and texting the other tenants of Brambleberry House, inviting them down to share after Skye was in bed.

Both Rosa and Sonia arrived at the same time, moments after her text went out. The three of them sat out in her screened porch, enjoying the evening breeze and the promise of rain.

"This is...delicious," Sonia said in her slow, halting

voice. She gave one of her rare smiles. "Thank you for inviting me."

"You're welcome."

"What brought on your frenzy of baking?" Rosa asked. "Not that I would be complaining, only curious."

Melissa couldn't tell them she had been restless for two days, since leaving Eli at A Slice of Heaven. "We went to the farmers market in Portland yesterday, and the strawberries were so luscious I couldn't resist buying four quarts of them. I have to do something with all those berries."

"Shortcake…was a great choice," Sonia said.

When Melissa offered the invitation, she hadn't really thought their second-floor neighbor would join them, but every once in a while Sonia did the unexpected.

The woman was such a mystery to her. Melissa had tried to gently probe about what medical conditions she had, but Sonia was apparently an expert at the art of deflecting conversation away from herself.

Why did she keep to herself? What secrets lurked beneath her pretty features? Had she been abused? Was she in hiding?

Melissa didn't feel darkness in Sonia's past, only… sadness. She couldn't explain it rationally, it was just a sense. There was a deep sorrow in Sonia. She wished she could get to the bottom of it.

Sometimes she thought becoming a nurse had heightened her compassion for others, giving her instincts she didn't fully understand. Her hunches had been proved right too many times for her to question them any longer, though. Now she simply listened to them.

Fiona, who had trotted down from the third floor with Rosa, lifted her head at that moment and seemed to stare off at nothing in the corner, head cocked as if listening to something only she could hear.

A faint hint of roses seemed to stir in the air, subtle and sly, but that might have been her imagination.

She followed the dog's gaze, then turned back to the other two women. "Do you ever get the feeling we're not the only ones in this house?" she asked impulsively.

"What do you mean?" Sonia asked, brows furrowed. For one brief instant, she looked so panicked that Melissa regretted bringing it up.

"Just… I sometimes feel like the house is alive with memories of the past."

"I know what you mean," Rosa said with her slight Spanish accent. "I never feel like it is malicious or scary."

"No," Melissa said. "I find it comforting, actually. Like somebody is watching over the house and those who live here."

"I don't believe in guardian angels," Sonia said flatly. "I wish I did. At times in my life, I could have used…a guardian angel…or two or twenty."

Her eyes looked haunted, and Melissa wanted to hug her, but she sensed Sonia wouldn't welcome the gesture.

"My grandmother used to say our family is always watching over you, whether you want them to or not."

"Don't you find that a little disturbing?" Melissa asked Rosa.

The other woman laughed and ate more of her strawberry shortcake. "Maybe. My mama's Tio Juan Carlos was crazy. I don't want him anywhere watching over me."

"It's not your crazy great-uncle. I get the feeling it's someone kind. Does that make me as crazy as Juan Carlos?"

Rosa smiled. "A little. But I am crazy, too. Maybe Abigail, the woman who lived here all her life and died when she was in her nineties, didn't want to leave. She's the one who left the house to my aunt Anna and to Sage Spencer. It could be she's sticking around to keep an eye on things."

"I remember Abigail a little from when we first moved to Cannon Beach," Melissa said. "I like the idea of a sweet older lady keeping watch over the house she loves."

"I do, too," Sonia said. "It's comforting, somehow."

While they finished their strawberry shortcake, they talked about the house and its history, what little Rosa knew from her aunt anyway. Eventually, the conversation drifted to men.

"How are things with the ex-husband?" Rosa asked. "Any updates after your frustration the other day?"

"No. I haven't heard from him."

At Sonia's questioning look, she explained the situation with Cody to the other woman.

"Who was that...good-looking guy I saw you with... yesterday?"

So much for keeping Eli out of her head for five minutes. She fought down a sigh. "That's my new boss. Dr. Sanderson's son, Eli."

"Oh! That's Eli! Wendell...said he might be coming home."

Melissa hadn't realized her neighbor was such good

friends with the elder Dr. Sanderson. As far as she knew, Sonia had only visited Dr. Sanderson once since she had been working there. It made sense, though, since he was the best doctor in town.

"If he's that cute, maybe I need to schedule a physical or something," Rosa teased.

"I think…I might be due for a follow-up appointment too," Sonia said.

It was the first joke she had ever heard the other woman make. Rosa looked just as surprised, then grinned. "Maybe we should just drop by the clinic this week to take Melissa out to lunch. We can check him out then."

"Good idea," Sonia said with what could almost be considered a smile.

"You're both terrible. Here. Have some more shortcake."

The conversation drifted to Rosa's work managing her aunt Anna's gift store in town and then to Sonia's plans for the garden.

"This was fun," Rosa said a short time later, stifling a yawn. "But I have to run down to Lincoln City first thing tomorrow to pick up some pottery from one of our suppliers. I had better get to bed."

"Same here," Sonia said. "Thank you for the dessert…and the…conversation."

She rose in her wobbly way.

"It was fun," Melissa said. "We should get together more often. Maybe you two could come for pizza night on Friday. Skye would love hosting a dinner party."

Sonia took on that secretive look she had sometimes.

"I won't be here this weekend. But maybe the week after that."

Where do you go? she wanted to ask her secretive neighbor. *And why are you so sad when you return?*

"I'll be gone, too," Rosa said with regret in her eyes. "Fiona and I are going hiking with some friends next weekend."

"No problem. We'll do it another time. Maybe the week after that, then. Put it on your calendars."

"Done," Rosa said with a smile.

"I'll have to look at my…schedule," Sonia said.

She said goodbye to them both, then made her slow way out of the screened porch and to the entryway that led upstairs to her own apartment.

"I hate watching her make that climb," Melissa said. "Why wouldn't she take the ground-floor apartment? It would be so much easier."

"I do not think that one wants the easy," Rosa said, her Spanish accent more pronounced. She stood up, and her dog rose, as well.

"And you don't know anything more about her…issues?" Melissa asked.

"No. She has been in town longer than I have, about four years. Anna said she showed up in town one day and started coming into the gift shop, mainly to pet Conan. That was the dog my aunt and Sage inherited from Abigail, who left them the house. Fiona's sire. One day she asked if Anna knew of any place in town she could rent, and it happened the apartment she lives in now was available. My aunt said she knew of one but it was on the second floor of an old house, and Sonia said it would be perfect. She has been here ever since."

One day Melissa wanted to get to the bottom of Sonia's mystery, though she knew it really wasn't any of her business.

After she said goodbye to Rosa and her dog, she straightened the kitchen, prepped a few things for breakfast in the morning, then headed to her solitary bedroom.

The apartment seemed too quiet and her mind was a tangle, wondering about Cody's plans, about Sonia's secrets, and about the disturbing knowledge that when she awoke, she faced an entire day of working in close proximity to Eli.

She dreamed that night that she was trapped on one of the rock formations off Cannon Beach in the middle of a storm. She was hanging on by her fingernails as waves pounded against the rock and a heavy rain stung her face. She was doing all she could to hold tight, to survive. And then suddenly Eli was there, shirtless but in a white lab coat with a stethoscope around his neck, like something off a sexy doctor calendar.

She might have laughed at her own wild imagination if she hadn't been so into the dream. "I've got you," he murmured in a throaty bedroom voice, and then he lifted her up with those astonishing muscles he had developed since leaving town. A moment later, she was in his arms and he was holding her tightly.

"I won't let you go," he promised gruffly, then his mouth descended and he kissed her fiercely, protectively.

Her alarm went off before she could ask him how

they were going to get off the rock and why he needed a stethoscope but not a shirt.

She awoke aroused and restless to a fierce rain pounding the window, as if she had conjured it with her dream.

It took her a moment to figure out where her dream ended and where reality began. What was wrong with her? She had been divorced for three years, separated for longer, and had told herself she was doing just fine putting that part of her life away for now while she devoted her energies to raising Skye.

Since the divorce, she had dated here and there but nothing serious, only for company and a little adult conversation. She hadn't been out at all since she came back to Cannon Beach.

She was lying to herself if she said she didn't miss certain things about having a man in her life. Topping the list would probably be having big, warm muscles to curl up against on a cool, rainy morning when she didn't have to get out of bed for another half hour. She sat up, wrapping her blanket around her, trying to push away the remnants of the dream.

Her wrist inside the brace ached, but it was more a steady ache than the ragged pain she had experienced over the weekend, further proof that it was only a sprain and not a break.

She looked up at the ceiling, listening to the rain click against the window. She didn't have to get Skye up for another hour, so she decided to stretch out some of the kinks in her back and the tumult lingering from that dream with her favorite yoga routine, making concessions to work around her sore wrist.

It did the trick. By the time her alarm went off, signaling it was time to wake up Skye and start their day, she felt much more calm and centered, and that unwanted dream and the feelings it had stirred up inside her mostly subsided.

She would simply ignore whatever was left, she told herself, just as she planned to ignore this inconvenient attraction to Eli.

The word *ignore* became her watchword over the next week. She managed to put aside her growing attraction to Eli, focusing instead on work and her online coursework and Skye.

She wouldn't exactly call this a good thing, but it helped that the area had been hit with an onslaught of fast-spreading spring viruses and a nasty case of food poisoning from bad potato salad at a spring church potluck.

They were insanely busy all week. Most of her time away from work was spent studying for final exams in the two online classes she had been struggling with, which left her little time to think about anything else.

Her relationship with Eli around the office was cordial and even friendly, but she tried hard not to let the ridiculous crush she was developing on him filter through.

By Friday morning, her wrist was almost completely back to normal except for a few twinges, and Melissa was more than ready for the weekend. It was her late day to go into the office and she decided to again take a quick run after she saw Skye off on the school bus.

She called Rosa to ask if she minded her taking Fiona.

"No!" Her friend said. "You will be doing me a huge favor. My day is shaping up to be a crazy one and I don't know when I will find the time to walk her."

A moment later, she and Fiona were heading out through the beach gate on the edge of the Brambleberry House garden, then running across the sand.

The water was rough this morning, the waves churning with drama. Clouds hung heavy and mist swirled around the haystacks offshore. She wanted to sit on the beach and watch the storm come in, but she had to finish her run in order to make it back for work.

As she and Fiona trotted down the beach, she spotted a few beachcombers and other joggers out. A couple holding hands stopped every once in a while to take selfies of each other and she had to smile. They were in their sixties and acting like newlyweds. For all she knew, they were.

She and Fiona made it to the end of the beach. As she neared home, she spotted a familiar figure running in the opposite direction with a little black schnauzer.

Eli.

This time, she gave him a friendly wave as she approached him, ignoring the nerves suddenly dancing in her stomach. His usually serious expression seemed to ease a little when he spotted her, but she wasn't sure if that was her imagination or not.

He slowed and Max and Fiona sniffed each other happily. "Looks like we're on the same running schedule."

"At least on Fridays. I don't get out as often as I like. The later opening for the office helps since I can go after Skye catches the bus."

"That must make it tough, trying to work out around her schedule."

"It wouldn't be as tough except I'm a wimp and only run when the sun is shining, which hasn't been very often this week."

She didn't want to talk about her sketchy workout habits. She'd done yoga twice. Counting that and her run a week ago when she'd met him on this very beach and today, that made four days in a week. That had to count for something, didn't it? Especially when she had an injury.

"How is your dad?" she asked to change the subject. "When do the doctors say he can go home?"

"He's doing great. The orthopedic doctor says maybe this weekend, but for sure by the middle of the week."

"That's terrific. I can only imagine how tough it must be to have double knee replacements, but I'm sure he'll be happy he did it."

"He already says it's less pain than he was in before."

The sun peeked through the steely clouds to pick up highlights in his hair. She ignored that, too—or at least she tried to tell herself she did.

"How's your wrist?" he asked. "I've been meaning to ask, but things have been so crazy this week as I try to settle in that I keep forgetting."

"It's been a wild week, you're right. You are getting a baptism by fire. We haven't been this busy in a long time."

"How did I get so lucky?"

She smiled. "Maybe all the women in town just want to meet the young, handsome new doctor."

He made a face. "Nice theory. It doesn't explain the food poisoning or the stomach bugs."

"Good point," she said.

Before he could respond, a cry rang out across the beach.

"Help! Please, somebody, help!"

For a split second, Eli went instantly on alert, muscles taut as he scanned the area.

An instant later, he took off at a dead run toward the older couple Melissa had seen earlier. Max wanted to chase after him, thinking it was a game, but Melissa took a moment to secure both dog leashes. As she sprinted after Eli, she saw the woman was kneeling beside the prone figure of her male companion, who was lying just at the spot where the baby breakers licked at the sand.

"What happened?" Eli was asking as he turned the man over to keep his mouth and nose out of the sand and the incoming tide.

"He was just standing there and then he fell over, unconscious. Please. What's happening?"

The man didn't appear to be breathing and his features had a gray cast to them. Melissa suspected a heart attack, but she didn't say so to the woman.

"What can I do?" she asked Eli.

"Help me move him up the beach, out of the water," Eli said urgently. The two of them tugged the unresponsive man six or seven feet up, just far enough that he wouldn't continue being splashed by the incoming breakers.

"Call 911," Eli instructed to Melissa as he started doing a quick first-aid assessment.

Adrenaline pumping, Melissa pulled out her phone and did as he asked.

"Does your husband have any history of heart trouble?" she asked while waiting for the dispatcher to answer.

"No. None," she said.

"Nine-one-one. What's your emergency?"

"We've got a nonresponsive male approximately sixty-five years old..."

"Sixty-seven," the woman said, her gaze fixed on Eli and her husband.

"Sixty-seven. He has no history of heart trouble but apparently collapsed about one to two minutes ago. Dr. Eli Sanderson is here attending to the patient, currently starting CPR. We are on Cannon Beach, near the water's edge about three hundred yards south of the access point near Gower Street. We're going to need emergency assistance and transport to the hospital."

"Okay. Please stay on the line. I'm going to contact paramedics. We'll get them to your location as soon as we can."

"Thank you."

"He's a doctor?" The man's wife was staring at Eli with astonishment filtering through her shock and terror.

"He is. And I'm a nurse. It's lucky we were here."

"Not luck," the woman said faintly. "It's a miracle. We were going to go up to Ecola State Park this morning beachcombing, but when we were in the car, something told me to come here instead."

They hadn't saved the man yet. She wasn't willing to go that far. "My name is Melissa and this is Eli."

Though that adrenaline was still pumping through her, she spoke as patiently as she could manage. The woman would have plenty of time to break down later, after the paramedics took over the situation, but right now it was important to keep her as calm as possible under the circumstances.

"Ma'am, what's your name and what is your husband's name?"

"Carol," she said faintly. "Carol Stewart. This is my husband Jim. We're from Idaho. The Lewiston area. We've been here for three days and are supposed to go home tomorrow. Today is our w-wedding anniversary."

Oh, she really hoped Eli and the paramedics could resuscitate the man. It would be utterly tragic for Carol to lose her husband on their anniversary.

"How long have you been married?"

"Th-three years. Three amazing years. It's a second marriage for both of us. We were high school sweethearts but went our separate ways after graduation. I got divorced ten years ago and his first wife died about five years ago, and we reconnected on social media."

"Is your husband on any medication?"

"High blood pressure and reflux medication. I can't remember which one, but I have the information on my phone."

"You can give it to the paramedics when they arrive."

Carol gave a distracted nod, her hands over her mouth as she watched Eli continue compressions without any visible response. "Oh, what's happening?"

Before she could answer, the dispatcher returned to the line. "Okay. I have paramedics on the way. They should be there shortly. I'll stay on the line with you until they arrive."

"Thank you. I'm going to hand you over to the patient's wife so she can answer any questions about his medical history for you to pass on to the emergency department at the hospital."

She turned to the other woman and handed over her phone. "Carol, take a deep breath, okay? I need to help Dr. Sanderson right now and someone has to stay on the line with the dispatcher until the paramedics get here. Will you do that for your husband?"

Melissa could see shock and panic were beginning to take over as the reality of the situation seemed to be becoming more clear. The other woman had turned as pale as the clouds, and her breathing seemed shallow and rapid. Carol took one deep, shuddering breath and then another, and appeared to regain some of her composure.

"I… Yes. I think so. Hello?"

When she was certain Carol wasn't going to fall over, offering them an additional patient to deal with, Melissa knelt beside Eli, who was giving rescue breaths.

"Any response?" she asked quietly.

He returned to his chest compressions without pause. "Not yet," he said, his voice grim.

"Do you need me to take over and give you a break?"

"Not with your bad wrist. I'll continue compressions, but it would help if you handle the respirations."

She moved to the man's head and the two of them worked together, with Eli counting out his compressions, then pausing for her to give two breaths.

She wasn't sure how long they worked together. It

seemed like forever but was probably only five or six minutes before she spotted paramedics racing toward them across the sand.

In the summertime, this beach would have had lifeguards who could have helped with the emergency rescue, but the lifeguard stations had personnel only during the weekends in May, then daily from June to August.

She knew both the paramedics, she realized as they approached. One, Tim Cortez, had gone to high school with both her and Eli and the other was a newcomer to town but someone she had actually socialized with a few times at gatherings, Tyler Howell.

She had found him entirely too much like her ex-husband, with that same reckless edge, and had declined his invitation to go out. Fortunately, he hadn't been offended and they had remained friends.

Two more paramedics she didn't know were close behind them.

"Hey, Melissa. Hey, Eli," Tim said as they rolled up. "What's going on?"

Eli was still counting compressions so Melissa spoke up to give the situation report. "We've got a sixty-seven-year-old man, Jim Stewart, with no history of heart trouble, on blood pressure and reflux medication. He collapsed about seven minutes ago and has been unresponsive since then but has been receiving CPR since about a minute or so after he fell over."

"Lucky for this guy, you two were close by," Tim said. "We've got the AED now. You want to do the honors, Eli?"

"I'll keep doing CPR while you set it up," Eli said.

A moment later, the paramedics had the automated external defibrillator ready. Eli stopped compressions while they unbuttoned the man's shirt and attached the leads.

Seconds later, Eli turned on the machine and followed the voice commands. A medical degree wasn't at all necessary to run an AED, but Melissa was glad she didn't have to do it.

The man shook a little when the electrical pulse went through him, shocking his heart.

When it was safe, the machine ordered them to check his pulse, and Eli felt for it. He grabbed a stethoscope that one of the paramedics handed over and listened for a heartbeat.

"Nothing," he said grimly. "We're going to have to do another round."

He resumed compressions while waiting for the machine to power up again, then stood back to allow the paramedics to reattach the leads and went through the process again.

Again, Jim's body shook, and Carol let out a little moan. Melissa went to her and put her arm around her as Eli again searched for a pulse.

"I've got something," he said, his voice containing more emotion than Melissa had heard since they had rushed to the man.

He listened with the stethoscope. "Yeah. It's getting stronger."

Both paramedics looked stunned, and Melissa couldn't blame them. She hadn't expected Jim to survive, either. Not really. If she were honest, she had suspected a massive heart attack, possibly even the kind they called the widow-maker.

"Nice work, Doc," Tyler said. He fastened an oxygen mask over Jim's mouth and nose.

Eli stood out of their way and let the two paramedics load Jim onto a gurney. Beside her, Carol was shaking.

"That's good, isn't it? That his heart is working again?"

She didn't want to give the woman false hope. Her husband wasn't out of the woods yet, not by a long shot, though he was starting to regain consciousness.

"Yes. So far, so good. The nearest hospital is up the coast in Seaside, about a fifteen-minute drive from here. That's where the paramedics will take him first. From there, they may decide he will need to go to Portland."

"Can I ride in the ambulance with him?"

She looked at Tyler, who nodded.

"I'm going to give you my contact info," Melissa said. "Where is your phone? I can enter it in for you. When you need a ride back to Cannon Beach, either to go to your hotel or to get your vehicle or whatever, you call me. I'll come pick you up and bring you back here."

The other woman burst into tears and hugged first Melissa and then Eli. "You've been so kind," she said as she quickly handed over her phone to Melissa. "Thank you. Thank you so much for what you've done. You're a miracle. Both of you. A miracle!"

Melissa was typing the last number of her contact info into Carol's phone when the paramedics started carrying the gurney since the usual wheels wouldn't work well on the sand.

"Let us know how things go with you."

"I will. Thank you."

A moment later, she and Eli stood alone.

"You didn't ride with him," she observed, a little surprised.

"The paramedics had things under control, and I would have just been in the way while they do their thing. I can put my ego aside enough to be sure that the cardiac specialist at the hospital is in a better position to treat Jim than I would be right now."

They both walked to where the dogs were tied up, and Melissa could feel her knees tremble in reaction.

"That was a little more excitement than you probably bargained for this morning," Eli said as he gripped Max's leash.

She patted Fiona's soft fur, wishing she could kneel right there in the sand and bury her face in it for a moment while she regained her composure.

"I would say the same to you. Way to step up, Dr. Sanderson."

"Part of the job description. You help where you can."

"It's more than that for you, isn't it? Even if you weren't a doctor, you're the kind of guy who would jump in and help in any emergency. You must get that from your dad."

He looked surprised by her words and, she wanted to think, pleased, as well. "I don't know about that. I do know that was probably enough of a workout for me today. I'm going to be buzzed on endorphins for at least another hour or two."

"Same here. I need to go." She smiled a little. "I'm

supposed to be at work in an hour, and my boss won't be happy if I'm late."

"Sounds like a jerk."

"He's okay," she said.

There was far more she wanted to say, but she didn't trust herself. She had just watched him work tirelessly to save a man's life and she wasn't sure she had the words to convey how much that had moved her.

Chapter Five

His hands were shaking.

Eli gripped Max's leash with one hand and shoved the other in his pocket, hoping to hell Melissa didn't notice.

They had just saved a man's life, and the reaction to that overwhelmed and humbled him.

This wasn't the first time he had saved someone's life. He had been a combat physician and had worked in some nasty hot spots all over the world. For several years, his focus had been refugee camps and providing help and education in war-torn villages, where his patients were usually light on hope and heavy on physical ills from all they had endured.

His efforts weren't always successful.

Too often, there was nothing he could do.

He knew that was the reason for his physical reaction now that the crisis had passed.

Somehow he had traveled back in his memory to the last time he had performed CPR on someone. When he had desperately tried to revive Justine even as he watched her life seep away.

He hadn't really expected Jim to survive. CPR didn't always work and even AED machines couldn't always shock a person's heart back after it had sustained significant damage.

He didn't know what Jim's chances were for long-term recovery, but at least his heart was beating on its own now. Eli had to be grateful for that.

He tried to blink away the image of Justine, of Miri, of those others who had been injured in that suicide bombing, but they remained burned in his mind.

That time, the outcome had been far different. Miri had died instantly. He had known the moment he had raced onto the scene. Justine had survived only moments, conscious and in agony for perhaps thirty seconds after he arrived, until she stopped breathing.

Despite all his efforts, despite the full hour of compressions he had done as they transported her to the makeshift refugee-center hospital. He had done CPR long after his arms started to burn with agony and his back muscles cramped.

The hell of it was, he had known almost from the beginning that she would not survive, and still he had tried. How could he have done anything else?

He let out a slow breath, aware of the cold, hollow ache in his stomach.

"You okay?" Melissa asked as they approached Brambleberry House, her forehead wrinkling with concern as she studied him.

"Fine."

She gave him a searching look but didn't call him on his short answer, which she had to know was a lie. "I'm glad you are, because I'm a wreck," she said instead, with a ragged-sounding little laugh.

"Why?"

"I only wanted to take my favorite dog out for a run. I never expected to play a small part in saving someone's life."

"Not a small part," he corrected. "You were fantastic. You kept Carol calm, focused the dispatcher and helped with rescue breathing when I needed it. We made an excellent team."

She looked surprised and pleased at the completely warranted praise. "Thanks. I'm just glad I was there so I could help. I think the remainder of today is going to seem a little anticlimactic, don't you?

"Probably."

"If only I could persuade my ogre of a boss to give me the rest the day off."

"If only he wasn't such a jerk and you didn't have a full caseload of patients today, he probably would have been happy to give you some time off."

"I guess we'll never know," she said as they reached the beach-access gate leading into the Brambleberry House gardens.

Her humor made him smile. For some reason he didn't quite understand, that made him feel guilty about

Justine and Miri all over again. It didn't seem right that he could smile and joke with a beautiful woman who made him desperately want to forget.

Some of his emotional turmoil must have shown on his features.

"Are you sure you're okay? You don't seem as happy as I might have expected, considering a very fortunate man is alive because of you."

He didn't speak for a long moment, unable to articulate the morass of emotions inside him. He should make some excuse and be on his way. If he wanted to stop at the hospital in Seaside before seeing patients, he had to hurry.

Still, he wanted to confide in her, for reasons he didn't wholly understand.

"This morning seemed to dredge up some things," he confided. "The last patient I performed CPR on didn't make it."

"Oh, Eli," she said. Her expression was drenched with compassion. "I'm sorry. That must be tough. But I can honestly say, seeing you in action today, I'm positive you did everything you could."

Had he? He wanted to think so but wasn't sure he would ever be convinced of that.

"You understand that not every battle we fight as health care professionals can or should be won," she went on softly.

"Yeah. I know. There have been plenty of times when I've had to accept I can't change the inevitable and that it is not in the patient's best interest to try." He paused. "It's harder when it's someone you know.

"The person you lost was someone you cared about."

He didn't know how she could possibly know that, yet she spoke the words as a quiet statement, not a question.

"Yes." He was appalled when emotions welled up in his throat, making it impossible for him to force any more words out around them.

"I'm sorry," she murmured again. She placed her hand on his arm in a small gesture of comfort.

"Thanks," he answered, more touched by her compassion than he could ever say. "I thought I had dealt with it, but apparently not."

"You didn't show your reaction when it mattered, in the heat of the moment, when you had work to do. I was right there beside you and had no idea what you were going through. You were professional, composed, in full command of the situation. I imagine that's something they teach you in the military. Do what has to be done when it matters, then react later."

"I guess."

"Was it another soldier you lost?"

He gripped Max's leash a little more tightly. "Justine was an aid worker. She was from a small town outside Paris, a doctor with Doctors Without Borders, in the last refugee camp where I was helping out. We…became friends."

More than friends, but he didn't want to tell Melissa that now.

"She died in a suicide bombing at a market square along with fifteen others." Including Miri. Sweet, smiling, innocent Miri. "I was a few hundred yards away when it happened, first on the scene."

"Oh, Eli. I'm so sorry. That must have been so difficult."

He acknowledged her sympathy with a nod. "It was. The situations aren't the same at all, except for the CPR part. For some reason, that brought everything back."

"Will you be okay?"

He forced his features into a smile, wishing he hadn't brought the subject up at all. "I'm fine. Thanks for worrying about me."

"In your professional opinion, Dr. Sanderson, is it appropriate for us to hug? I could sure use one, after everything that's happened this morning."

He didn't consider himself necessarily a physical person, but he really craved the comfort of Melissa's arms right about now. "I could use one, actually."

He wrapped his arms around her and she sagged against him with a little sigh, wrapping her arms around his waist.

It felt so damn good, warm and personal and kind. He had needed a hug for a long time.

He and Justine hadn't been in love. She was more concerned with saving humanity than starting up a relationship with him or anyone else. Still, their relationship had been a bright, happy spot in a miserable situation, and her death had filled him with a complex mix of guilt, grief and deep regret that her shining light to the world had been extinguished.

Melissa's arms tightened around him and she rested her head against his chest, soft and sweet and vulnerable.

After a few more moments, his sadness seemed to trickle away, replaced by something far more dangerous.

Maybe this hug between them wasn't such a good idea. His body was suddenly reminding him that he was still very much alive, and he could think of several excellent ways to reinforce that.

She made a soft, breathy sound and his groin tightened. He'd had a thing for Melissa for a long time. Having her in his arms now was better than anything he could have imagined.

And he shouldn't be here.

"I should, uh, probably go," he said.

She sighed and stepped away, and he instantly wanted to gather her close again. It was only a simple embrace. Why did it fill him with such peace?

"I'm proud of what you did. You saved a man's life, and I was honored to be part of it." She smiled a little and, before he realized what she intended, she stood on tiptoe and kissed the corner of his mouth.

For a moment, he stood frozen, stunned into immobility. Her lips were soft and tasted like strawberries and cream, his very favorite dessert. He felt her breath on his skin, warm and delicious, and the heat of her where she stood close to him.

More.

That little taste wasn't enough. Not by a long shot. She eased her mouth away after that first little brush of her lips against his. He wasn't fully aware of moving his mouth to more fully meet hers, but he must have. One moment her lips were barely touching the edge of his mouth, the next he had turned his head so that he could capture her mouth in a true kiss.

She made a little sound in her throat, a gasp or a sigh,

he wasn't sure which, and her breath seemed to catch, then she kissed him back. Her arms were still around his waist from their hug and now they tightened, pulling him closer.

She was the most delicious thing he'd ever tasted, and the sweetness of her kiss and the incredible *rightness* of her arms around him seemed to wash over Eli like cleansing, healing rain. He kissed her with an urgency bordering on desperation, afraid he would never have the chance again to stand with her between the ocean and a flower garden, afraid he would never again know a kiss like this, one that moved him to his soul.

He should *not* be doing this.

The thought whispered to him over and over, quietly at first, then with increasing intensity.

She worked for him. For his father, technically, but right now for him. This was highly inappropriate, and he needed to stop this moment.

He started to pull away, but she made a soft, sexy little sound and pressed her body against him, as if she couldn't bear to let him go. It was like a match held to dry kindling, the only spark needed for him to ignite. He deepened the kiss, pulling her tightly against him.

He wanted her more than he remembered wanting anything in a long time.

All week as they had worked together, he had been trying not to admit that to himself. He had forced himself to view her strictly as a colleague, a nurse whose dedication and abilities he admired.

Now he could admit he had been lying to himself. Now, with her here in his arms, he could no longer deny it. He saw her as far more than that.

He had a thing for Melissa Fielding and had from the time he was eighteen. She had been the prettiest girl in town, with her big green eyes and her generous smile and the kindness that had always been part of her.

He couldn't have her then because she had eyes only for the jock and popular kid, Cody Fielding.

He couldn't have her now because of a hundred different reasons, mostly because he couldn't be the kind of man she needed.

All those reasons he needed to put a stop to this now, before things skyrocketed out of control, raced through his brain, and he tried to find the strength to heed the warnings. He couldn't do it. She felt too damn right in his arms, as perfect and lovely as a spring morning on Cannon Beach.

She was the one who finally pulled away, easing her mouth slowly from his, her breathing ragged and her eyes dazed and aroused.

A mischievous wind seemed to slide around them, warm and rose scented, though that didn't make sense since it was too early for roses in the Brambleberry House gardens by about a month.

Eli lowered his arms from around her, the magnitude of what had just happened hitting him like a huge Japanese glass fishing ball dropped from the highest branches of the big pine tree on the edge of the garden.

He had just kissed Melissa Blake Fielding—and not a simple kiss, either, but a hot, passionate, openmouthed kiss that couldn't be mistaken for anything but what it was. A clear declaration that he wanted her.

"That was...not supposed to happen." Her voice sounded breathless, thready, sexy as hell.

"Agreed." He ran a hand through his hair, not sure how to respond.

"I'm not completely sure what *did* happen," she admitted. "I meant to just kiss you on the cheek and then somehow...things sort of exploded."

He had wanted them to explode. Something about the emotional turmoil of the morning had lowered all his defenses, allowing heat and aching hunger to filter through.

"We have both just been through something intense. Sometimes when that happens, when adrenaline spikes and then crashes, people can react in strange ways."

"That must be it." She didn't look particularly convinced and he couldn't blame her. He had been through plenty of intense things in the military and had never used that as an excuse to tangle tongues with anybody else.

"It was extremely inappropriate of me to kiss you," he said, his voice stiff.

"Was it?" She blinked, clearly at a loss to understand what he meant.

He sighed and took a step farther away, though he knew the opposite side of the beach wouldn't be far enough to make him want her less.

"Technically, I'm your boss. You work for me. In some corners, this might be considered workplace harassment."

She stiffened. "We are not in the workplace right now. And for the record, you did not harass me. I kissed you first."

"A kiss on the cheek. And then I turned it into something else."

"I wanted you to," she admitted. "I kissed you right back. Did you miss that part?"

He frowned. "It still shouldn't have happened."

"Maybe not, but nobody harassed anybody. And technically, I work for your father, not you. You're just the substitute doctor."

He gave a half laugh, not sure whether to be relieved or offended. "You're right. I'm leaving again as soon as my dad is on his feet."

Her features froze for a moment, then she gave a tight smile. "End of story, then. It happened, we can't change it, so let's just move on from here."

He sighed, not knowing what else to say. "Right. Well, I apologize for any inappropriateness on my part and promise it won't happen again."

Again, she offered that tight smile. "Great. Now I really do need to get going. You might not be justified in firing me because of the way I kiss, but you could if I'm an hour late to work."

"This morning's events more than excuse your tardiness."

"I'll let you try to get that one past Carmen and Tiffany," she said. "I'll see you at work."

He waited until she and her neighbor's dog moved out of sight before he gripped Max's leash and hurried toward his father's house, wishing he had time for a quick jump in the cold Pacific before he headed into the office.

Chapter Six

Though she wanted to find a nearby bench in the beautiful gardens at Brambleberry House and just collapse into a brainless, quivering heap, Melissa forced herself to keep walking toward the house, afraid Eli somehow might be watching.

The kiss they had just shared had shaken her to her core. The heat of it, the intensity behind it, the emotions stirring around inside her. Who would have guessed that Eli could kiss a woman until she couldn't think straight?

Her knees were trembling like she'd just run a marathon, and it was taking every ounce of concentration she had to stay on the path and not to wander blindly into the lilac bushes.

Oh. My. Word.

Dr. Sanderson Jr. packed one heck of a wallop in his

kiss. She had been so very tempted to stay there in his arms for the rest of the day and simply savor the magic of it.

He was right, though. Their kiss was a mistake that never should have happened. At the first touch of his hard mouth on hers, she should have come to her senses and realized what a disaster this was.

She still wasn't sure why she hadn't done exactly that. Maybe it was the adrenaline crash from working on Jim, or maybe it was the highly inappropriate dreams she was still having about him, or maybe it had simply been the result of the long week of doing her best to fight her attraction to him.

Regardless, their kiss *had* happened. How on earth was she supposed to face him at work all day without remembering the taste of his mouth or the salty, musky scent of him, or the safety and security she found in his arms?

She had a serious crush on the man. This morning hadn't exactly helped her gain control of it, first watching him save a life and then sharing that amazing kiss.

As she headed with Fiona toward the house, Rosa walked out on the back porch to greet her. She could tell immediately that her friend had seen her and Eli together at the bottom of the garden. She must have been sitting here when they walked up, with a clear view down to the garden to the beach-access gate.

The only thing she could do was own it. "Yes. Okay. I just kissed my boss. We're both determined to forget about it. I would appreciate if you would try to do the same."

Rosa gave a laugh that she tried to disguise as a cough. "All right. Enough said. It's none of my business anyway."

Okay, she probably shouldn't have said anything. Now she'd only made things worse by bringing attention to the kiss, like in high school when girls used to walk into class and announce to everyone that they had a new pimple.

"Sorry," she mumbled.

"Nothing to apologize for. I only came for my dog so you did not have to walk her up the stairs."

"Thanks. You have no idea what kind of morning it's been. Eli and I happened upon a tourist who collapsed from a heart attack."

"Is that what the paramedics were doing? I heard the sirens and worried. How is he?"

"Better than he would have been if we hadn't been there. Eli gave him CPR, then shocked him with the AED and he came back. It was amazing to see."

"I can imagine. Good for Eli."

"The kiss you saw. That was kind of a crazy reaction to what happened. The adrenaline rush and everything. We shouldn't have… It won't happen again."

"We are not going to talk about that, though." Rosa smiled and Melissa felt a wave of gratitude for her.

"When do you leave for your hiking trip?" she asked.

"The plan was to take off tonight and be back tomorrow night, but my friend just texted me and had an emergency in the family, so now we're leaving tomorrow and will be back Sunday night. Fiona will be here until then, just in case you need her."

"I might. Thanks."

Fiona tugged at her leash, obviously wanting to be home, and Rosa gave the dog an exasperated look. "I'd better get her some water, then we've got to head into the office. Have a good day."

"Same to you."

As Rosa and Fiona headed up the stairs to her apartment, Melissa opened the door to her own.

Inside, she fought the urge to collapse on her bed for a few hours. Or maybe the rest of the day.

Rosa had wished her a good day. She had a feeling it would be anything *but* good. How on earth was she supposed to make it through, especially having to face Eli again after that stunning kiss?

She could do it. She had tackled tough things before and she could do it again.

No matter how difficult.

By some miracle, she and Eli managed to get through the day's appointments at the clinic without too much awkwardness between them.

Melissa had decided on a strategy of avoidance. Though it was tough, she tried to pretend their kiss had never happened, that they hadn't spent a glorious five minutes with their mouths tangled together and his arms tightly around her.

It was one of the toughest things she'd ever had to do. Every time she passed him in the hall or shared an exam room with him while he spoke with a patient, she had to actively struggle to keep from staring at his mouth and remembering the heat and magic of their embrace.

The only saving grace was the clinic's caseload. They were both busy with patients all day and didn't have time for small talk. She almost made it through her shift without being alone with him, until she waved goodbye to Carmen and Tiffany and headed out to the parking lot at the end of the day, only to find Eli walking out just ahead of her. She almost turned around to go back inside but couldn't think on her feet quickly enough to come up with an excuse.

She found her urge to flee annoying and demeaning. So they'd shared a kiss. That didn't mean she had to be uncomfortable around him for the rest of his time here in Cannon Beach.

She put on a cheerful smile. She could do this. "Do you have big plans for the weekend?" she asked, then instantly regretted the question. She did *not* want him thinking she was hinting that they should get together or something.

He shook his head. "Dad is hoping he'll be ready to come home soon, so I'll probably be busy making sure the house is ready for him. What about you?"

"Not really. Skye and I are running into Portland tonight to take Carol's things to her. The hotel has already packed them all up for her."

"That's very nice of you."

"It's the least I can do."

Jim had been airlifted to the hospital in Portland and Carol had flown with him, unwilling to leave his side even long enough to come back to Cannon Beach for their suitcases.

"What's the latest? Have you heard? When I talked

to Carol earlier, she told me he was likely going to need a quadruple bypass."

"Then you know as much as I do. The surgery won't be until tomorrow, from what I understand. I feel good about his chances, but it's too early to say if he's out of the woods."

"At least he *has* a chance. He wouldn't have, if not for you."

"And you," Eli said.

It was a shared bond between them, one she never would have expected when she awoke that morning.

He smiled a little, more with his eyes than his mouth. Melissa fought a shiver. She also wouldn't have expected that kiss.

Why had he kissed her? And would it happen again?

She cleared her throat. "I'd better go. Skye will be waiting for me at the babysitter's."

"Right. Pizza night. Tell her I meant my invitation of the other day. The two of you are welcome to come to my dad's house so she can shoot some pool. Nobody else is using it. Who knows, maybe she can turn into a pool shark and start fleecing all the tourists over at A Slice of Heaven."

"You're a bad influence on my child," she said, shaking her head. And on *her*, she wanted to add, giving her all kinds of ideas she didn't need complicating her world right now.

She had a weekend away from him to regain her perspective, and the sooner she started the better chance she would have of putting that kiss out of her head.

She gave him a wave and had started to climb into

her SUV when another vehicle pulled into the parking lot—a flashy red convertible carrying two people, a blond male and a darker-haired, more petite female.

She paused, ready to explain that the clinic was closed. The convertible pulled up next to her. When the driver pulled off his sunglasses and climbed out with athletic grace, Melissa let out an involuntary gasp.

"Cody! What…what are you doing here?"

Her ex-husband beamed his trademark smile that had appeared on surfing magazine covers for more than a decade. "I told you I was working on coming back to Oregon. And here I am."

"I didn't realize you meant you were coming back immediately."

"I wanted to surprise you, Missy."

"I'm surprised, all right." She couldn't have been more surprised if he'd come back to town with tattoos covering his face like a Maori warrior. "Are you…moving back to Cannon Beach?"

"No. We're just here hanging out with my buddy Ace. You remember him, don't you?"

"Oh, yes." Ace had been a jerk in high school and now had a string of used car lots along the coast. From what she heard, he was *still* a jerk.

"We're going to settle in Portland, near my folks. Since I lost my sponsorship, I need to find a more reliable paycheck. Got that baby on the way and all. My dad's been pushing me to join his office and this seemed as good a time as any."

Now he wanted to be financially stable? For the five

years they had been married, he had been perfectly content to let her support them with her nursing career.

"You're going into real estate." She tried to process that shocking information, but it was too much for her brain, after the day she'd had.

"I guess I have to pass some kind of class and stuff before I can actually do any selling. But I'm going to start small and see where it goes."

Knowing her ex as she did, she had no doubt he would probably be brilliant at it. Cody had always been good at convincing people he had exactly what they needed.

After her dad died, Cody had been so sweet and attentive, making her feel like the most important person on earth. She had been grieving and lost, and he had helped remind her the world could still have laughter and ice cream and sweetness.

"You know how you've been bugging me to spend more time with Skye. This is my chance! We're moving into one of my dad's rentals in Portland and working out of his office there. We'll only be a few hours away."

"Great."

"Amalia can't wait to meet her. She's been asking every day."

"Amalia."

"My wife. That's one of the reasons I stopped by before we go out to dinner with Ace and his wife. I want you to meet her. Babe, get out here."

A young woman who looked to be in her early twenties rose from the passenger seat of the convertible with a grace that matched Cody's. She was dark and petite, tanned and fit and gorgeous. And very, very pregnant.

"Oh." The word escaped before Melissa could swallow it down.

Cody glowed like *he* was the pregnant one. He held out a hand to the woman, who moved to his side looking elegant and beautiful—so different from the way Melissa had looked when she was pregnant with Skye, when her ankles had disappeared and all the baby weight had somehow settled in her hips and butt.

"This is Amalia. I met her in Brazil. She doesn't speak much English."

"Hello, Amalia."

"'Ello." The woman's voice was low and throaty and exotic, though she looked nervous. Cody didn't speak a word of Portuguese, as far as she knew. If his new wife didn't speak much English, Melissa had to wonder how they communicated.

"Like I said, she's been dying to meet Skye. Where is she?"

"Not here," she said, pointing out the obvious. "This is my workplace. She's at the babysitter's."

"Oh. Right." He gave a little laugh. "I should have realized that. Where does the babysitter live? I can go see her there."

Skye would be thrilled to see her father. She adored him despite his chronic negligence.

"It would be better if I picked her up. Why don't you meet me at Brambleberry House in about an hour. Do you remember where that is?"

"I think so. Sounds good."

He started to lead his wife back to the car, then apparently noticed Eli, still waiting and watching the scene beside his father's Lexus SUV.

Cody's gaze narrowed. "You look familiar. Have we met?"

Eli coughed politely. "Yeah. Eli Sanderson. We went to school together. You and some buddies ambushed me in the parking lot once during a school dance."

Cody let out a rough laugh. "You're kidding me. Why would I do that?"

Eli shrugged. "You apparently weren't very happy with me for asking Melissa to dance."

"Kind of a dick move, dude, asking another guy's date to dance with you."

"Sometimes. In this case, I guess I figured you wouldn't care, since you had been ignoring her all night."

Cody laughed out loud at that. "I was an ass in high school. I hope there are no hard feelings."

He was *still* an ass, on many levels. She couldn't believe it had taken her so many years to figure it out.

"Why would there be?" Eli said coolly. "It was a long time ago."

She had completely forgotten about that school dance. As usual, Cody had abandoned her in the corner while he talked to his friends. She might as well have been invisible for all the attention her date paid her that night. That wasn't a unique situation. Even now, she wasn't quite sure why she had put up with it for so long.

"Anyway, we're staying the night at Ace's guesthouse, but I was hoping we could take Skye back to Portland with us tomorrow."

"Why?"

"We're buying some things for the new little munchkin, and I figured she might like to be involved in the whole baby thing."

As usual, he didn't think about anyone but himself. He didn't consider that she might have plans with her daughter. They were just supposed to drop everything for him.

According to the Gospel of Cody, the world revolved around him and always would. She hated thinking of the years she had wasted trying to make things different.

She glanced at the pregnant young woman beside him, who looked at Cody like he was the sun and the moon and the stars, all wrapped up in one perfect man.

She wanted to tell him to forget it, that she and Skye would be busy, but her daughter truly did adore her father and she would be sad to miss the chance to spend time with him.

"I'm sure she will be happy to see you."

The truth was, Cody wasn't necessarily a bad father. He did love their daughter, she just didn't come first, the way a child should.

"Perfect. We thought we would leave about eleven."

"I'll have her ready."

"Maybe we'll just wait until then to have Ami meet her. Save us time tonight, since we have to get ready for dinner. Does that work?"

"It should be fine."

"Thanks, Missy. This is gonna be great. You'll see."

With that use of the nickname she hated, he helped his pregnant young wife into the passenger seat of his impractical little red sports car, hopped into the driver's seat and pulled out of the parking lot, leaving Melissa feeling as if she had just been pounded by heavy surf against a seawall.

She closed her eyes for a moment, then opened them, wishing she could have dealt with that encounter alone, without any witnesses.

"Well, that seems like a pretty sucky way to start a weekend."

Eli's dry tone surprised a laugh out of her. "Congratulations, Dr. Sanderson. You officially get the understatement-of-the-week award."

"I was talking about me. It's tough being confronted with the guy who once tried to beat me up."

"Tried to?"

"I was tougher than I looked even when I was a tall, awkward geek."

He had *never* been awkward. She remembered that now, too late.

"I studied jujitsu from about age nine and had a few moves that still serve me well." He studied her. "I take it you're not exactly jumping for joy about your ex-husband's return. Is it the pregnant new wife?"

"No. Not exactly. Skye will be thrilled about having a new sibling to love and she'll be over the moon that she might see Cody more often. She loves her father."

"That's the important thing then, isn't it?"

His words struck with the ring of truth. "Yes. Thanks for the reminder."

He studied her for a moment, blue eyes glinting in the fading sunlight. "You've got your hands full tonight and don't need a trip to Portland. Why don't you let me take care of Jim and Carol's suitcases tonight?"

"I offered. It doesn't seem right to hand off the duty to you simply because it's become inconvenient."

"I don't mind. Max loves riding in the car, and it will give me the chance to check on my patient."

He was such a good man. Why couldn't she have seen past the skinny geekiness when she had been in high school instead of being drawn to the macho, sexy surfer type? She could have avoided so much heartache.

"That's very kind of you. They were staying at The Sea Urchin. The innkeeper has already packed up their suitcases for them. Thank you, Eli."

"It's no problem," he assured her. He gave her a smile that almost reached his eyes this time, and she surrendered even more of her heart to him.

He made it extremely difficult to resist him, and she was completely failing at the task.

"Didn't you say he was coming at eleven? That was forty minutes ago. Where is he? Do you think he forgot?"

Melissa could feel the muscles in her jaw ache and forced herself to unclench her teeth. "He'll be here," she assured her daughter, though she wasn't at all positive that was the truth.

As she looked at Skye watching anxiously out the window, Melissa was painfully reminded of all the nights she had waited for Cody to come home or call from the road when he said he would.

Cody was great at making promises and lousy at keeping them.

"He'll be here," she said again. "Let me text him again and see where he is."

She quickly shot off a text, only refraining from swearing at him by the same superhuman effort she was using to keep from grinding her molars.

It took him several long moments to reply.

Running late. Waves too good this AM at Indian Beach. On way now.

That was more of an explanation than she used to get from him but still not enough to placate a girl who adored him.

"Looks like he's on his way. Do you have everything you need to sleep over? Pajamas, a change of clothes, your emergency phone, some snacks, coloring paper and pens, your American Girl doll?"

"Yep. Got it all." Skye gave her gap-toothed grin, and Melissa's heart gave another sharp tug. She loved this kind, funny, creative little person with all her heart.

Her daughter was growing up. What would the future hold for this sweet, openhearted child?

"Why don't you practice your reading with me for a few more minutes while we wait?"

"Okay." Skye picked up the book she was reading about a feisty girl who resembled her greatly. They were both laughing at the girl's antics when the doorbell rang.

"That's him!" Skye exclaimed. She dropped the book and raced to the door eagerly.

It was, indeed, her father. Cody walked in with his exotically beautiful bride silently following along.

"Great place." Cody gave an admiring look around the big Victorian, with its high ceilings, transom windows and extensive woodwork. "I remember this from when that old biddy Abigail What's-Her-Name lived here. She never liked me."

"It's been a good apartment for us. The other tenants are wonderful and the landlords have been more than accommodating. It has worked out really well while I continue trying to save up enough for our own place."

"When you're serious about looking, make sure you let me help you. Who knows? I might even discount my commission."

She dug her nails into her palms and forced a smile, when what she really wanted to do was roll her eyes and remind him that if he were more dependable with child support, she could have bought a house when she first came back to town.

"Wow. Thanks. You might want to get your real estate license before you go around making that kind of generous offer."

"Working on it. Working on it. You ready, Skye-ster?"

"Yep." She threw her arms around Melissa's waist. "Bye, Mommy. Love you."

"Bye, sweetie."

"I'll bring her back tomorrow afternoon. Not sure what time. I was thinking we could maybe hit a baseball game in the afternoon."

No problem. She had nothing else to do but sit around

and simply wait for him to drop off their child whenever he felt like it.

"Sounds like fun," she said, forcing another smile. "When you figure out your plans, I would appreciate a text or call so I know roughly when to expect you."

"You got it. Thanks, Missy."

He picked up Skye's suitcase and the booster seat she claimed she didn't need anymore but legally did because she was small for her age. At least Cody didn't argue about that as he led the way back to his flashy convertible. The booster seat barely fit in the minuscule back seat.

She stood on the sidewalk, watching as he helped Skye buckle in, opened the door for his new wife, then climbed in himself.

As Cody backed out of the driveway, Melissa whispered a prayer that her baby girl would be okay, then headed into her empty apartment.

Her remaining chores went quickly, especially without Skye to distract her with hugs and stories and eager attempts to help.

At loose ends, she couldn't seem to focus on her own book or on the television series she was working her way through on Netflix. If only her mother were in town, they could go for a long lunch somewhere, something they never seemed to have time to do.

She needed physical activity but couldn't summon the energy required for a run. After dithering for a few more moments, she finally decided to take a walk to deliver one of the loaves of banana nut bread she and Skye had made earlier that morning to her friends Will and Julia Garrett.

On impulse, she texted Rosa at work, asking if she was still around and, if so, could Melissa borrow Fiona for a walk.

Rosa immediately texted back a big YES with four exclamation points. Then she added, Both of us would thank you for that.

She smiled a little through her glum mood, grateful all over again that her wanderings had led her back here to this beautiful house and new friends.

She had a key to Rosa's apartment, and Fiona jumped around excitedly when Melissa reached for her leash by the door.

"I'm taking a treat to the neighbors," she informed the dog. "You can only come along if you promise to behave yourself. They've got that handsome Labrador who is nothing but trouble."

Fiona shook her head as if she disagreed, which made Melissa truly smile for the first time since she had watched a red convertible drive down the road.

As she and Fiona walked down the stairs, she momentarily thought about inviting Sonia along, then remembered the second-floor tenant was out of town on one of the mysterious trips she took.

Every few months, an anonymous-looking car-service limousine would pick her up and Sonia would slip inside carrying a suitcase, then would return again by another limousine three or four days later.

Rosa had once asked her where she went, but Sonia, as usual, gave vague answers. She had offered some excuse about having to go away on a family matter, then had quickly changed the subject.

Considering she claimed she had no family, that excuse made no sense, but neither she nor Rosa had wanted to interrogate her about it.

The April afternoon was sunny and lovely, perfect for walking, with a sweet-smelling breeze dancing through the Brambleberry House gardens and the sound of waves in the distance.

She wanted to enjoy it and was annoyed with herself that she couldn't seem to shake this blue mood.

Unfortunately, when she and Fiona walked the three blocks to Julia and Will's beautifully restored home, nobody answered the door. She knocked several times but received no answer.

Too bad. She should have called first to make sure they were home. She could always freeze the banana bread, she supposed, though it was never quite as good as when it was fresh out of the oven.

She took a different way home, not realizing until she was almost to it that her route took her directly past Wendell Sanderson's house. She wouldn't have intentionally come this way, but apparently her subconscious had other ideas.

A sharp bark greeted them, and Fiona immediately started wagging her tail and straining at the leash when she spotted Max just inside the garden gate…in the company of Wendell's entirely too appealing son.

She really should have taken another way. Oh, she hoped he didn't think she was staking out the house in the hopes of seeing him.

She couldn't just walk on past, as much as she wanted

to. Eli watched her approach, a screwdriver in his hand and an expression on his features she couldn't decipher.

"Hi," he said.

She gestured to the gate. He was installing some kind of locking mechanism, she realized. "This looks fun."

"Since my dad's surgery, Max has decided he's the canine version of Houdini. He's learned how to open the latch and take off."

The dog looked inordinately proud of himself.

"Oh, how sweet. I bet he's letting himself out so he can go look for your dad!"

"That is entirely possible. Or maybe he just doesn't enjoy my company."

That is not *possible*, she wanted to say, but didn't have the nerve.

"How is your dad? When is he coming home?"

"Not as early as he'd hoped. He's been doing so well, we thought he might be cleared to come home tomorrow, but I guess yesterday he had a little tumble during physical therapy."

"Oh, no!"

"He seems to be all right, but the doctor at the rehab center wants to keep him until at least Monday or Tuesday, to be safe."

"I'm sorry. That must be disheartening for both of you, especially if he thought he was going home sooner."

On impulse, she held out the loaf of banana bread. "Will you take this to him? Skye and I made it this morning for Julia Garrett and her family, but they're not home. Your dad particularly enjoys our banana nut bread."

Eli looked astonished. "Thanks. That's very kind of

you, but are you sure you don't want to save it and give it to your friend later?"

"Banana bread is best when it's fresh. When Skye gets home from Portland, we'll make another batch."

"Portland. I forgot she was going with her dad. How are you holding up?"

"Super," she lied. "Except I couldn't stand how quiet my house was, so I borrowed my neighbor's dog and went for a walk so I wouldn't have to be alone there."

He smiled a little at that and patted Fiona, who gazed up at him with adoration.

She had been holding back her emotions all day, but the kindness in his eyes seemed to send them bubbling over. To her great and everlasting dismay she sniffled a little, a tear dripping down her cheek.

"Hey now. It's okay," Eli said, looking slightly panicky. "She won't be gone long."

"I know. She'll be back tomorrow."

Melissa felt so stupid! It was only an overnight visit. Fiona licked at her hand and it was the absolute last straw. She sniffled again and before she knew it, Eli had set the loaf of banana nut bread on top of the gate and reached for her, pulling her against his hard muscles.

"It's okay," he said again.

"She's never been away from me. Not one single night. She's seven years old and she's never slept somewhere she couldn't call out to me. Her father has taken her before but only for a few hours at a time. He doesn't know that she needs a night-light on and she has bad dreams if she eats too much sugar past eight, and when she wakes up, she does this sweet little stretchy thing."

"He'll figure all that out. The important parts anyway."

She let out a sigh, wishing she could stay here the rest of the evening so he could help keep her nerves away. "I know. You're right."

"Cody loves Skye, right? You said as much yesterday."

"He does. He doesn't always do things the same as I would, but that doesn't mean he doesn't love her."

"They will be fine. Skye strikes me as a clever girl. If there are any problems, she can always give you a call to come get her."

This was dangerous, being close to him like this. She couldn't help remembering their kiss the day before, and the way she had flung her arms around his neck and surrendered to her overpowering attraction toward him.

Holding him like this, being close to him and hearing his heartbeat against her cheek, was entirely too risky. It was making her think all kinds of wild thoughts. She was aware of a soft tenderness blooming to life inside her like the spring growth all around them. He was so kind, so concerned about her feelings. He made her feel like she mattered.

How was she supposed to resist that?

She had to. He was leaving again. He'd told her so himself. She couldn't afford to lose her heart to a man destined to break it into a thousand pieces.

Though it made her ache inside to do it, she forced herself to step away. "Thank you. I'm sorry you had to talk me down off the ledge."

"You're welcome. Anytime." He studied her. "You know what you need tonight? A distraction."

For one crazy second, her mind went into some completely inappropriate directions. She could come up with some pretty delicious ways to distract herself involving him, but she had a feeling that wasn't what he was talking about. "What did you have in mind?"

"Tiffany from work and her band are playing at The Haystacks tavern tonight. She gave me a flyer yesterday on her way out the door. I was thinking it would be nice to support her."

Melissa tried not to wince at the suggestion. She adored the young CNA for many reasons, but her musical ability wasn't among them.

"You haven't heard her sing, have you?"

"Is it that bad?"

"Taste can be such a subjective thing."

"In other words, you hate it."

"I don't hate it, exactly. Her band's style is what you might call an acquired taste."

"Well, hers isn't supposed to be the only band. According to the flyer, there are two other bands playing after hers. Who knows, we might get lucky and one might even be tolerable. What do you say?"

Why was he asking her? Because he felt sorry for her? Was he only being kind, or did he also dislike being alone on a Saturday night?

Did his reasons really matter? She didn't want to stay at home by herself watching television and feeling sorry for herself. He was offering a perfect distraction. If she didn't go, she would be alone all evening, without even Fiona for company, since Rosa was leaving town.

"I suppose it would mean a lot to Tiffany if we both came out to listen to her."

"There you go. A night on the town, plus supporting a coworker. You can't lose."

She wouldn't go that far. There was always the chance she would end up letting down her guard too much and inadvertently reveal the big crush she had on her boss.

She would simply have to be careful that didn't happen. The benefits of getting out of the house offset the small risk that she might make a fool of herself.

"What time?"

"Does eight work?"

"Yes. It's a d—" She caught herself before she said a word that rhymed with eight. This was *not* at date. They were simply two coworkers going out on the town to support someone else who worked with them.

"Deal. It's a deal," she improvised quickly. "Eight works for me."

"Perfect. I'll pick you up then."

"Great. Meantime, I hope your dad enjoys the banana nut bread. If you're lucky, he might even share some with you."

"I'll keep my fingers crossed."

She smiled, grabbed Fiona's leash and headed back toward Brambleberry House, feeling much better about the world than she had a few moments earlier.

Chapter Seven

As he drove up to the big, sprawling Victorian house where Melissa lived with her daughter, Eli was aware of a vague sense of danger.

He knew it was ridiculous. He had been in war zones, for heaven's sake, in countless hair-raising circumstances. He had operated on people with bullets flying, had jumped out of helicopters into uncertain territory, had tried to provide medical care in villages where he knew armed hostiles were hiding out.

Yeah, those things had been terrifying. Melissa Blake Fielding posed an entirely different sort of threat.

The woman got to him. She always had. He'd had a thing for her all those years ago when he was in high school, and apparently the intervening years had done nothing to work it out of his system.

This wasn't a date, despite the flowers on the seat next to him. They were friends and coworkers, he reminded himself. He had no intention of making things more complicated with her.

Sure, he liked her. The pretty cheerleader she had been in school had grown into a woman of strength and substance, someone who showed compassion and kindness to everyone.

She hadn't kissed him out of kindness. His abdominal muscles tightened at the memory of her sweet response the day before and the eagerness of her mouth against his. She had been as into the kiss as he was. He knew he hadn't misread the signs.

That didn't change the fact that he never should have let things go as far as they had.

Melissa had become an indispensable part of his father's practice. His father had told him how very much he relied on her. Eli had no business coming into town for a few weeks and messing with the status quo simply because he wanted something.

This wasn't a date, and he needed to remember that he wasn't the kind of man she needed. He couldn't be that man. She needed someone focused on home and family, not somebody who was simply marking time until he could go back and finish the job he had left undone overseas.

He found deep satisfaction working for the Army Medical Corps. He was helping other people and making a difference in the world, in whatever small way he could. Since Justine and Miri had died in that market square, however, his responsibilities had taken on vital urgency. Justine had been a dedicated physician, passionate about providing care to the desperate and helpless. He felt driven to continue her work.

Her life had held purpose and direction. Her death—and Miri's—had been meaningless, the result of a cruel, fruitless act of violence. He was the trained military officer, and he should have picked up on the signs of unrest they had seen when they entered that village. He should never have let her go to the market that day. Instead, he had ignored his instincts and she had died as a result.

Because of him, she would no longer be able to help anyone, and he felt a sacred obligation to continue his own work in her memory. What else could he do?

He wasn't free to let himself fall for Melissa, no matter how attracted he was to her. It wouldn't be fair to either of them.

He wasn't in love with her. They'd only kissed once, for heaven's sake. She was his coworker and his friend.

He was half-tempted to throw the flowers his father had insisted he bring into the garbage can over there, but that would be wasteful. Friends could bring friends flowers. That didn't mean this was a date.

With that reminder firmly in his head, he walked up the porch steps of Brambleberry House and rang the doorbell just as another woman trotted down the steps carrying a backpack, with Fiona the Irish setter on her leash.

The woman was pretty, with warm brown eyes and wavy dark hair. She stopped and smiled at him, eyes widening a little when she spotted the flowers. He tried not to flush but had a feeling he wasn't very successful.

"Hello. You must be Dr. Sanderson's son. Eli, right? The army doctor."

What had she heard about him? And from whom? Had Melissa mentioned his name? He sighed, annoyed with himself. This wasn't junior high. It didn't matter if Melissa had mentioned him to her friend or not.

"That's right."

"Nice to meet you. I'm Rosa Galvez. I live upstairs, third floor."

"Any relation to Anna Galvez?" he asked as he petted the dog with his free hand.

Rosa nodded. "She's my aunt, sort of. I was adopted by her brother and his wife, anyway, when I was a teenager."

He sensed a definite story there, especially when the warmth in her eyes seemed to fade a little.

"Anna was always kind to me when I used to go into her gift shop. I understand you're running the place now."

"That's right. I love it," Rosa said. "How is your father doing?"

He couldn't go anywhere in town without people asking him that question, but Eli didn't mind. It was further proof of how beloved Wendell was around Cannon Beach.

"Okay. He had a little setback yesterday, but he should be home soon. The knees are better than ever, he says. Soon he'll be ready to chase all the ladies again."

She smiled. "Give him my best, will you? I like him very much. Your father, he is truly a good man and a good doctor."

"I'll tell him. Thank you."

"You are here to see my friend Melissa, no?"

"Yes. That's right." He found her trace of Spanish accent completely charming.

"Her doorbell is that one."

"Thanks."

She paused and appeared to be debating whether to add something. In the end, she gave a quick glance at Melissa's doorbell, then looked back at him. "I am glad you are here for Melissa tonight. She is having a struggle right now. It is hard to share a daughter."

"I imagine it would be."

"Thank you for being her friend. I am glad to know Dr. Sanderson's son is a good man like his father."

Was he? He was completely positive his father wouldn't have kissed one of his nurses until neither of them could think straight.

Fiona tugged on the leash before he could answer, and Rosa laughed a little. "I have to run. We are off on a little adventure and she is a little excited about it."

"Safe travels," he said.

"Thank you."

She hurried down the steps toward an SUV parked next to Melissa's vehicle, loaded her dog and backpack quickly and backed out.

At least the unexpected conversation had helped put the evening in perspective. Melissa needed a morale boost, and he was glad he had the chance to offer one.

He rang the doorbell, his hands tightening around the flowers in his hand.

When Melissa opened the door, his breath seemed

to catch in his chest and, for a crazy moment, he forgot why he was there.

Friends, Eli reminded himself. They were only friends.

"Hi."

"Hi, yourself."

He couldn't think what to say for a long moment, then he remembered the flowers. "Here. These are for you. Peonies from my dad's garden. He was thrilled with the banana bread. It's one of his favorites. When I told him we were going to listen to Tiffany tonight, he insisted I cut some flowers to pay you back for the bread. They were my mom's favorite. The peonies, I mean."

Okay, he was babbling. He never babbled.

She looked touched by the gesture. "He showed me a picture of your mother once. I wish I'd known her. She had the kindest eyes."

He felt the pang he always did when he remembered his mother, the ache that had become a part of him after all these years. "She did."

"How old were you when she died?"

"Twelve."

"I'm sorry. That must have been rough. I was fourteen when I lost my dad. The pain never quite goes away, does it?"

He shook his head, aware of yet another thread tugging him toward her. They both knew the void left behind from losing a parent at a young age.

He didn't know what to do with this soft tenderness unfurling inside him so he focused on the flowers, instead. "Anyway, the vase is from my dad. He made it in ceramics class at the rehab center. He wanted you to keep it."

Her features softened. "I'll cherish it even more, then. It's lovely. I have to tell you, I adore your father. If only he were thirty years younger!"

"Not the first time I've heard that phrase since I've been back in Cannon Beach," he said ruefully. His father was quite popular with women of all ages in town. Somehow Wendell managed to make every woman feel like she was the most important one in his world.

"Come in a moment while I find somewhere for these and grab my purse." She opened the door, and he followed her into the apartment.

He didn't know what the apartment had looked like before she moved in, but it was clear Melissa and her daughter had turned the space into a home. A large dollhouse stood in one corner, with a baseball bat propped against it and several stuffed animals on the roof, as if keeping watch. The room was cheery and open, with splashes of color from prints on the wall and bright pillows on the sofa and chairs.

"What a great view," he said, immediately drawn to the wall of windows facing the ocean.

"Killer, isn't it?" She moved to stand beside him and admired the rugged coastline outside the sunroom. "This is my favorite spot in the house. Sometimes I can't believe I really live here."

He glanced down at her features, pretty and open and genuine, and had to battle down a fierce urge to kiss her again. It would be so easy. He only had to close the small space between them and lean his head down just so. He could almost taste her, fresh and sweet as ripe strawberries.

His head dipped slightly, but he checked the movement just before he would have followed through on the powerful urge.

No. They were friends. That was all they could ever be. Melissa had enough complications in her life right now with her ex-husband moving back. She didn't need somebody with Eli's kind of baggage.

He was aware of her small swallow, of the way her gaze shifted from his eyes to his mouth and back again so quickly he wondered if he had imagined it.

It wasn't a good idea to be here alone with her in her warm, comfortable apartment. Not when she was everything he wanted and everything he couldn't have.

"We should go."

Was that disappointment he saw in her eyes? No. He was imagining that, too.

"We should. We wouldn't want to miss Tiffany in all her glory. Just give me a minute."

"Great."

He turned back to the window, hoping he had the strength to keep his hands off her all night.

She wasn't sure why, but Eli Sanderson seemed as uncomfortable as she felt as they walked into The Haystacks tavern.

Why? If she was the reason, what had she done to make him so edgy?

She had a feeling he was regretting whatever impulse had prompted him to invite her out tonight to hear Tiffany's band. She should have backed out when she had the chance. She could have made up some excuse, but she had been so grateful for the distraction she hadn't really thought through how awkward Eli might find it to spend time socially, after their heated kiss the day before.

It was too late now. He had invited her and she had accepted. The only thing she could do now was to make the best of it and try to relax and enjoy herself.

"Have you been here before?" she asked.

He looked around the tavern, with its brick walls and weathered plank bar. "Not recently. I may have stopped in with friends a time or two when I would come back to town during college, but I didn't have a lot of time for barhopping."

The Haystacks was one of those rare drinking establishments that didn't try to be trendy or hip. Its simple unpretentiousness made it popular with tourists and locals alike.

"It's not a bad place. They host some fun events, and on Saturday nights they feature all local musicians."

The place was already crowded and Tiffany's band was setting up on the small stage in the corner of the tavern. Eli managed to find them a table near the stage. He pulled a chair out for her and waited until she was settled before he sat across from her.

"I probably should warn you, I'm not much of a drinker," he admitted. "I've seen too many guys who spent every moment of their R & R hammered."

"You might change your mind and order a drink once the music starts."

He laughed roughly, a sound that seemed to ripple

down her spine. "You've built it up so much, I can't wait."

"I shouldn't have said that. I'm sorry. Tiffany actually has an excellent voice. I'm just not sure Puddle of Love is the best venue for her talent."

"Her band is called Puddle of Love."

"I tried to warn you. It's not that bad. I'll be quiet and let you judge for yourself."

She ordered a mojito while Eli ordered one of the locally brewed ales.

She waved at a few people she knew from his father's practice and another couple who had gone to high school with her.

Their order came quickly. She sipped at her drink, then sat back in her chair. "Now that you've been here a week, what do you think?" she asked, making conversation. "Are you ready to stick around in Cannon Beach and go into practice with your dad?"

He shifted. "How did you know he was lobbying hard for that?"

She shrugged. "Lucky guess. I know how proud he is of you and how thrilled he is to have you back. It makes sense that he would want to make it permanent. He said your term of service is done but you're considering signing up for another few years."

He sipped at his beer, his gaze focused on the band setting up.

"Do you love the military that much?" She had to ask.

"It's not that I love it, necessarily. But I know I'm making a difference. I feel a certain…responsibility to continue doing what I'm doing."

"You could make a difference here, too."

"You make it sound so easy."

"Why isn't it?"

He was quiet, sipping at his beer again. "It's complicated."

"Doesn't seem like it to me."

"I'm good at what I do. I don't say that to be cocky, but there's something very fulfilling in knowing I'm helping people who have very few options available to them."

"I can see that."

"To be honest, I'm also not sure I'm ready to settle in one place. The idea of seeing the same patients day after day for the rest of my life seems so…final."

To her, that sounded like a dream come true. She yearned for roots. She had gone to nursing school before she and Cody were married and had barely earned her license before he decided it was time to move to Hawaii, where she had to retake her license requirements. They had lived in a half-dozen places during the five years they were married and she had to become relicensed three times.

She had loved staying in one place and having the chance to get to know their patients a little better.

She supposed everybody had different needs.

Before he could respond, Stew Peters, who ran the bar, went to the microphone. "Hey, everybody. Thanks for coming out. As you all know, it's locals' night tonight. Performing for the first time here at The Haystacks, give it up for Puddle of Love."

She and Eli clapped with enthusiasm as Tiffany took to the stage, looking far different from the young woman Melissa had seen the day before, leaving the office in blue scrubs and a ponytail. Oddly, she also didn't resemble the leather-clad, big-haired rocker Melissa had seen fronting the band the last time she had seen them, at a little dive in Manzanita before Christmas.

This time she was dressed in a simple flowered dress, with her multicolored hair pulled back in a modest headband. Except for the multiple piercings and the vivid hair, she looked like a coed who had stopped into the bar between classes.

She took the microphone and the band behind her started up. As Melissa looked closer, she noticed several significant changes. The drummer was the same, but the guy on lead guitar and the girl playing bass were new to the band.

Tiffany's look and the band personnel weren't the only changes. She could tell after the first few bars. Puddle of Love had mellowed their sound significantly, cutting down on the screaming, angry lyrics and allowing Tiffany's strong contralto voice to come through.

By the time her friend finished the first song, Melissa was clapping along with the rest of the tavern crowd.

"I feel like I missed something here," he leaned in to say when there was a break in the music. "Were you deliberately trying to give me low expectations? They sound great to me."

"This isn't the same Puddle of Love I've heard before, trust me. This is Puddle of Love 2.0."

"I like it."

"So do I."

They both settled in to enjoy the music, mostly covers of rock ballads that somehow sounded evocative and unique with Tiffany's voice. When the set finished, the medical assistant walked through the crowd, greeting people she must have known, until she came to their table.

She looked impossibly young. "You guys came. Wow! I never thought you would."

"I'm glad I got to hear you before I leave town," Eli said. "That was terrific. You've got a gift."

The nurse's aide looked at Melissa.

"I enjoyed every minute of it," she said honestly.

"Thanks, you guys. Seriously, thanks. I like working for your dad—it's a good job—but I kind of feel like I need to take a break from everything and put all my energy into this, you know?"

Melissa remembered being young and passionate, ready to put all her faith into helping her husband follow his dreams.

What about her own dreams? What had she wanted?

"My parents think I'm crazy," Tiffany said with a little laugh. "Do you really think we're good enough to go for it anyway?"

She asked the question of Eli, who looked uncomfortable at being put on the spot. "I'm, uh, probably not the best person to ask. I'm not very musical."

"But you know what you like, right? I saw you getting into the groove."

He looked to Melissa for help, and she tried to tell herself they weren't really a team even when it felt like they were.

"You guys were terrific, Tiff. Seriously. If this is what you really love, I say give it a try. You'll have another chance to get into nursing school, and you've already got your nursing assistant certification to help support you while you follow your dream."

As she spoke the words, she was fully aware of how hypocritical they were. She had given the same advice to Cody, to follow his dream and go for it, then had resented him for devoting all his time and energy to it.

It was too easy to fall into the trap of blaming all the problems in their marriage on his immaturity and lack of commitment. She held a fair share of the responsibility, had been completely unprepared when hard reality hadn't matched up to her rosy expectations.

Tiffany didn't need to hear that right now. Her friend glowed. "You're the best. Both of you! Are you guys staying for the next group? Glass Army is pretty good."

Melissa glanced over at Eli, who shrugged. "We've paid the cover. Might as well get our money's worth."

"Cool." Tiffany looked over her shoulder to where the drummer was gesturing to her. "Looks like J.P. needs me. Thanks again for coming. I'll see you guys Monday."

She gave Eli a radiant smile, hugged Melissa and returned to her bandmates.

Melissa sighed. "Did somebody just warp time in here? Because I feel about twenty years older than I did when we walked in."

He smiled. "I know what you mean. But for the record, you don't look a day older than Tiffany."

She told herself not to read anything into that. She picked up her drink again, determined to ignore the heat sizzling between them and focus on the music.

Chapter Eight

His date-who-wasn't-a-date was a little tipsy. She wasn't precisely drunk—she had only had two and a half mojitos over the past two hours—but he could tell she had let down some of her barriers and seemed more soft and relaxed than he'd seen her since he'd come back to town.

She yawned in the middle of a conversation about which band she preferred—Tiffany's, obviously—and he smiled a little. "We should probably get you home. It's late."

"I don't want to go home," she declared with a hint of defiance in her voice. "It's too quiet there."

The bar didn't close for another hour, but without the live music it had lost most of its appeal for him. Other than The Haystacks, the options for late-night entertainment in Cannon Beach weren't exactly what anyone could call extensive.

"I guess you're right, though," she said with a sigh. "We can't stay here all night."

She rose and started gathering her purse and the jacket she had brought along. She walked out to his dad's SUV with her usual elegant grace, but stumbled a bit when she reached to open the door.

"Here. Let me," he said.

She gave him a broad smile, another hint that she might not be completely sober. "You're just as sweet as your father. Don't tell him I said so."

"I won't," he promised. He made sure she had her seat belt on securely before walking around the vehicle, climbing in and starting it up.

"Oh, look at that dog," she exclaimed as they passed a late-night dog walker with a large yellow Lab on a leash. "I wish I had a dog. Too bad I can't borrow Fiona, but Rosa took her with her out of town. Everyone is gone."

She seemed genuinely sad, but that might have been the mojitos talking.

"Do you want to borrow Max for the night? I'm sure he would be happy to have a sleepover."

She leaned back in the leather seat. "Maybe." She closed her eyes. "He's so cute. He can sleep on the floor by my bed and warn me if any bad guys come around."

He had to smile a little at that and hope he didn't fall into that category. "He can be pretty fierce."

"That's what I need. A fierce dog like Max to protect me."

The idea of telling her he thought she needed a worn-out army doctor sounded ridiculous so he said nothing. "I'll stop at my dad's place and grab Max for you, and

I can swing by in the morning to pick him up. Does that work?"

"You are the best boss ever. I mean it. The best!"

He couldn't help the laugh that escaped. For some reason, she gazed at him, an arrested expression on her features.

"I wish you would do that more often," she said.

"What?" The word seemed to hang between them, shimmering on the air.

"Laugh. I like it so much."

He caught his breath, aware of a strange tug, a softness lodged somewhere under his breastbone. This was dangerous territory, indeed. This woman threatened him in ways he wasn't at all prepared to handle.

"I'll keep that in mind," he murmured.

She smiled and closed her eyes, leaning against the leather seat back. A few moments later she was asleep, her hands tucked under her cheek like a child's.

At a stoplight, he looked over, captivated by her. In some ways, she resembled the sweet-faced cheerleader he'd had a thing for back in the day, but he could see now that was an illusion. She was so much more. She had grown into a woman of character and substance, her world changed and shaped by life.

At his father's house, he paused in the driveway for a moment, wondering if it was a stupid idea to loan her Max for the night. She would be fine without him and might find the dog more trouble than he was worth. But Eli had promised. If she would find some solace and comfort from having another creature in the house, Eli wasn't about to stand in the way.

As for Max, the dog would probably treat the whole thing as a fun adventure. He'd been at loose ends with Wendell in the rehab center and would probably enjoy being needed again.

Max trotted up to him as soon as Eli walked inside, making it an easy matter to scoop up the schnauzer, his food and water bowls, his leash and his favorite blanket. He carried all of it back to his dad's vehicle.

Melissa was still asleep, her breathing soft and measured. After another moment's hesitation, he set the dog and all his comfort supplies on the back seat, then reversed out of the driveway to head the short distance up the hill to Brambleberry House.

If anything, Melissa seemed to have fallen more deeply asleep, snuggling into the leather of the seat. He turned off the engine, reluctant to wake her. He could see Max was snoring away in the back seat, too. Apparently, Eli's company wasn't very scintillating to anyone.

He smiled ruefully and sat for a moment in the stillness of the vehicle. The rest of the world seemed far away right now, as if the two of them and Max were alone here in this quiet, cozy little haven.

Outside the windows, he could see the glitter of stars overhead and the lights of Arch Cape to the south, twinkling against the darkness. A strange, unexpected sense of peace seemed to settle over him like a light, warm mist.

The night was lovely, the sound of waves soothing and familiar. Little by little, he could feel the tension in his shoulders and spine begin to ease.

This…

This was the calm he had been yearning to find since he returned to town. How odd, that he would discover it here in his father's vehicle with a snoring dog in the back seat and a beautiful sleeping woman in the front.

He wasn't going to argue with it. He was just going to soak it in while he had the chance.

Eli closed his eyes, feeling more tension trickle away. He hadn't even realized how tightly wound he had been, yet he found something unbelievably comforting about being here with her. He couldn't have explained it; he only knew she soothed something inside him that had been restless and angry for months and allowed him to set down the twin burdens of guilt and grief for a moment.

Like Max and Melissa, there was a chance he may have fallen asleep, too. He didn't intend to, but the day had been a long one and he felt so very relaxed here beside her.

He awoke sometime later, disoriented and stiff from the uncomfortable position.

Something was different. He opened his eyes and realized with some degree of wonder that she was in his arms.

How had that happened? He hadn't moved, was still behind the wheel, but now he held a woman against him. Her arms were around him, her head resting in the crook of his elbow, and he cradled her against him like a child.

He looked down at her lovely features, tucked against his chest, and was astonished at how absolutely right she felt in his arms.

No. This wasn't right at all. Hadn't he been telling

himself all night how he couldn't be the kind of man she needed?

None of that seemed to matter, not here in the darkness. Here, he could admit the truth he had been running from since he'd returned to town.

He was falling for her.

More accurately, he supposed, he was finally allowing himself to acknowledge that he had fallen for her a long time ago and simply had been biding his time, waiting for life and circumstances to bring them together again.

He didn't want to admit it, even to himself. What good would it do? There was no happy-ever-after in the stars for them. He had obligations elsewhere.

His heart ached at knowing this was all they could ever have, these few stolen moments together in his father's SUV in the darkness while the waves pounded relentlessly against the sand.

He wasn't sure if his sudden tension communicated itself to her or if he made some sound or perhaps the dog did, but she began to stir in his arms. She opened her eyes, and for one startling moment there was a blazing joy in her expression, as if she were exactly where she wanted to be, then she seemed to blink a few times and the expression was replaced with confusion and uncertainty.

"Eli. Wh-what are you doing here?" She sat up a little and pulled back to the passenger side of the vehicle, hands in her hair. "What am *I* doing here?"

"We went to see Puddle of Love, remember? Then we stayed for the next group and the next, and there's a chance you may have had a little too much to drink. You fell asleep as I was driving you home. I waited in the driveway for you to wake up but I must have fallen asleep, as well."

She looked out the window, where a light, misty rain had started to fall.

"Okay. That's embarrassing."

"For you or for me? You at least had a moderate degree of alcohol consumption for an excuse. I had one beer all night."

She looked around. "Alcohol or not, I'm still not sure what we're doing *here* in your SUV in the middle of the night. And how did Max get here?"

Quite clearly, he was the one who should be embarrassed about the situation. "You, uh, didn't want to sleep alone tonight so I offered to bring Max up to stay with you."

She shook her head, massaging her forehead. "Well, that will go down in history as one of the most awkward episodes I've ever had with a coworker."

She glanced at the clock on the dashboard. "Is it really after one?"

"Yes. If it's any consolation, I think we only dozed off for an hour or so."

"I should probably go inside. Either that or go down to the beach and dig a giant hole in the sand to climb into."

"You have no reason to be embarrassed, Melissa. Seriously. It was kind of sweet, actually."

He shouldn't have said that. He knew it the moment the words were out. She gazed at him, her blond curls tousled and her eyes soft and her mouth parted slightly. It was all he could do not to yank her back into his arms.

"I'll walk you in," he said, a little more gruffly than he intended.

"Thanks."

"Would you still like Max to stay with you for the night? I can take him home if you'd rather not bother."

She looked at the dog in the back seat, who was beaming at her with that goofy look of his. "I'd like to say no, but I would actually appreciate his company. Having him here might help the house not feel as empty."

He opened the rear door for Max, and the dog trotted up the sidewalk as if he owned the place. Eli grabbed Max's blanket, leash and bowls.

As they walked toward the house, she pulled out her key. "I'm suddenly starving. Are you hungry? I've got stuff on hand to make an omelet, if you want."

He was torn between his conviction that it wasn't a very good idea to spend more time with her and his overwhelming desire to do exactly that.

As if to seal the deal, his stomach suddenly growled and he realized dinner had been hours ago, before he picked her up to go to The Haystacks. He had nibbled a bit on bar snacks, but apparently that wasn't enough.

"There you go," she said with a winsome smile. "Come in."

"I can grab a sandwich at home."

"I'm not super talented in the kitchen, but I do make a mean omelet. They're kind of a specialty of mine. Come on. It's the least I can do, after you were kind enough to let me sleep in your car."

It would be rude to refuse, he told himself. Plus, he wanted to make sure she would be okay on her own without her daughter.

"An omelet does sound good right now."

She smiled and unlocked the door. "It will hit the spot. Trust me."

He did. He trusted her more than any woman in a long time.

The question was, did he trust himself?

What had seemed like a brilliant idea while the two of them were standing outside on her porch suddenly lost a great deal of its shine once they walked inside her apartment.

Melissa was having a hard enough time resisting the man. Sharing late-night snacks alone in her kitchen when there was a chance she might still be slightly buzzed could very well be more temptation than she could resist.

She was still trying to deal with how perfect it had seemed to wake up in his arms. She had felt safe and warm and cared for, though she knew that was ridiculous. How had she ended up there? She still wasn't quite sure. He had explained that she had fallen asleep in the vehicle on the way home from the tavern, but that didn't really explain how she had gone from sitting on her side of the vehicle to being cradled so tenderly in his arms.

Had she snored? Drooled? Done anything else completely mortifying? She had no idea. She also didn't understand how he had *let* her keep sleeping when he could have awakened her the moment he pulled up outside

Brambleberry House. Why hadn't he just honked the horn or shouted in her ear? He could have just opened the door and pushed her out, for that matter.

Still, waking up in his arms had felt completely right, somehow.

She was falling for him and she had no idea what to do about it. She knew perfectly well it would only end up in heartbreak for her. He had made it clear he was leaving at the first opportunity. Under other circumstances, she might have followed after him and used her own skills to help those in need.

That was utterly impossible at this stage of her life. She had a daughter. They were settling into life here in Oregon. She didn't have the freedom to let herself fall for someone whose heart was somewhere else. Been there, done that.

She swallowed. She had invited him for an omelet, which was the least she could do after he had been so sweet about trying to distract her from being upset about Skye spending the night with her father.

So she had slept in his arms for a few moments and had awakened with a powerful urge to kiss the dark shadow of his jaw and pull his mouth to hers. She hadn't done that, which meant she had more self-control than she gave herself credit.

She only had to keep her hands off him for the ten minutes it would take her to fix him an omelet and the ten minutes it would take him to eat it. She could handle that.

She led the way into the kitchen, flipping on lights as she went, and quickly tied on an apron.

"This won't take long," she promised him.

"I can help."

"There's not much to do. I suppose you could cut the peppers while I do the onions."

"Sure."

She pulled a green pepper out of the refrigerator, pointed him to the cutting board and handed him a knife, then put on the food-grade gloves she used so onion juice didn't seep into her skin.

After sniffing around it, Max settled into the corner on the pillow Skye kept there for Fiona's visits, and a comfortable silence filled the kitchen, broken only by the sounds of chopping.

She was the first to break it.

"Who is Miri?"

His knife came down hard on the cutting board, and if she hadn't been watching him she might have missed the sudden bleak look that he quickly blinked away.

"How do you…know about Miri?"

"I'm not sure. I think you may have said her name in your sleep. I thought maybe I'd dreamed it, but obviously not."

He let out a breath and then another, and she could tell the question had upset him.

"I'm sorry. I shouldn't have said anything. I was only curious. You don't have to tell me."

He turned his attention to briskly cutting the peppers. Any smaller and they would disappear in the omelet. After a moment, she took them from him and added them along with her chopped onions to the sizzling oil in the omelet pan.

The smells made her mouth water even as her attention remained focused on him.

"I told you about Justine the other day."

"Your doctor friend who died in the suicide bombing. Or was she more than a friend?"

"I'm not sure what we were," he admitted, confirming her suspicion. "We had dated a few times, if you can call it dating when you're in a war zone, surrounded by people facing starvation and violence."

"You said she was there with Doctors without Borders. What was your role? Can you talk about it?"

He hesitated for a moment, and she wondered if she had overstepped, then he spoke. "For the last twelve months, I've been deployed to the Middle East, providing medical care in various refugee camps and setting up clinics in small struggling villages trying to recover from decades of unrest."

"Not an easy task."

"I've been deployed most of the last five years. After the first tour, I asked to go back. It had its challenges but there were many rewards. These are courageous people who have already lost so much, facing truly horrible circumstances."

Every time she heard about people living in rough conditions like Eli was talking about, Melissa regretted her propensity to feel sorry that her life hadn't turned out the way she'd planned. She had so many amazing things in her world. She had a job she loved, good friends, a great apartment next to one of the most beautiful beaches in the world. No, things weren't perfect, but on the whole, her life was extraordinary.

"We were trying to improve conditions," Eli said. "I like to think we were making progress. Justine was absolutely dedicated to the cause and was a real inspiration to everyone."

Features pensive, Eli pulled Max onto his lap and scratched the schnauzer beneath his chin. "As you can imagine, the camp had more than its share of orphaned children."

"How sad." She didn't like thinking about children who had no one to love them.

"There was one in particular who always wanted to help the aid workers. She used to ask to sweep the floor of the medical clinic."

"Miri."

"Yes. She was about seven or eight, the sweetest girl, with a huge smile."

He let out a soft, tortured sigh. "Everyone in the camp watched over her, but she and Justine had a special bond. Miri used to bring her little bouquets of flowery weeds or pretty rocks she'd found. Justine wanted to adopt her, take her back to France with her, and was trying to put the wheels in motion."

She wanted to say how wonderful that such sweetness could survive the horrors of war, but she sensed she didn't want to hear what was coming next. She could see by the tension in his shoulders and the way he gripped his hands tightly together that the rest of the story wasn't as tender.

"What happened?"

She flipped the omelet, wishing she hadn't asked any questions and started them down this grim road.

"One day, Justine asked me to go with her to a village about five or six kilometers away from the camp to help with a clinic for pregnant women and children. A routine trip, we both thought, something we'd done a dozen times in other villages. It was well within my mission as part of a PRT, Provincial Reconstruction Team, trying to help these war-torn areas rebuild." He paused. "She thought it would be fun to take Miri with us. The girl was very good at putting villagers at ease and convincing them to trust us."

He was silent, his eyes haunted by memories she couldn't begin to guess at.

"I didn't want to, but it made both of them happy so I relented. I liked to see them smile. Miri had started doing it more and more, especially when all three of us were together."

"What happened?"

"It was market day and the area was busy. We didn't stop working all morning and saw maybe twenty women, but then things began to slow down a little. I… Miri and Justine decided to walk to the market square to grab some lunch for us and look at some of the local goods on sale. I should have said no, that we should stick together. I'd been uneasy all day, feeling a weird energy."

"Would Justine have stayed behind simply because you asked her to?"

He made a face. "Probably not. She was fiercely independent. If I had told her I had a weird feeling, she would have laughed at me and called me *Monsieur Poule Mouillée*."

"Mr. Wet Hen," she said, smiling at his quite excellent French accent. Hers wasn't great, but she understood better than she could speak from studying it in school.

"I told myself I was imagining things. There was no potential threat. Why would there be? We were aid workers. I stayed behind at the clinic and didn't go with them because I was too busy showering all my knowledge on the village's young, inexperienced midwife. I had just about run out of things to yammer on about when we heard the blast."

"Oh, Eli."

His features were grim. "Apparently, there were still opposition forces in the area angry that the leadership of this village would accept foreign aid workers. They killed fifteen villagers at a peaceful market square for no reason, along with a sweet orphan girl who only wanted to help."

"Miri," she whispered, heart aching for the devastation she heard in his voice.

"She died instantly. Justine was conscious and in agony for only a moment after I arrived on scene. I tried to stabilize her, but she'd lost too much blood and the shock was too great. She went into cardiac arrest. I told you I did CPR while we tried to call for help but… It was too late. I couldn't save either of them."

She had no words, nothing that could comfort this sort of deep pain.

"Miri was only a girl, with a future that was much brighter than it had been a few months earlier, before Justine came into her life. I hate knowing that future was wiped out because of me."

"Why do you blame yourself?"

"I could have made other choices. I shouldn't have let them go into the market alone. I should have been with them. We should have taken more protection with us."

"Could any of those things have stopped what happened?"

He looked helplessly at her and she knew the answer. No. He would have been a target, too.

She removed the omelet from the stove to a plate, choosing her words with care. "You can't blame yourself, Eli. You didn't plant the explosives and you couldn't have known someone else would. You were there to help people."

"I know that intellectually. Convincing my emotions isn't quite as easy."

The torment on his features broke her heart. She was a nurse, driven to ease suffering where she saw it, and she hated knowing she couldn't help him.

She couldn't resist going to him and wrapping her arms around his waist. She wanted to tell him not to blame himself, that she understood he had been there to help others and he couldn't hold himself responsible for the evil actions of a few, but she knew that would be cold comfort.

Still, something in her touch must have calmed him, as she hoped. After a few moments, she felt some of the tension in his muscles seep away. He returned her hug with a grateful embrace before he stepped away.

"I'm sorry. I keep thinking I've dealt with it. It was six months ago and most of the time I'm fine. Every once in a while, I let down my guard and the memories wash over me like a flash flood."

"I'm glad I was here to keep them from drowning you."

"So am I." He gestured to the table. "But I hate to waste a good omelet, especially when you've gone to all the trouble to make it. Should we eat?"

For all the sadness of his story, she found the meal surprisingly restful. They spoke of mutual acquaintances and some of the changes that had come over the town in the years since both of them had lived here. She didn't want their time together to end, but the long day finally caught up with her and she couldn't hold back a yawn.

He glanced at his watch, shook his head and rose. "I should go. It's nearly two. Thank you for the omelet and the evening. I enjoyed both."

"Thank *you.* I forgot all about missing Skye."

He shrugged into his jacket and headed for the door. She walked him there, with Max trotting at their heels.

"If you want to take Max home with you, I should be okay. I feel silly I was ever worried about being alone. This house just feels so big when I'm the only one here, especially when I know Sonia and Rosa aren't in town."

"Keep him until Skye gets home, if you want. He's good company. To be honest, you're better company to him than I will probably be. He's been lonely, I'm afraid. I think he misses my dad. And I'll be at the rehab center most of the day, so he would be alone otherwise."

He planned to spend his Sunday with his father, which filled her with a soft tenderness. "You're a very sweet man, Eli."

He raised an eyebrow. "Why? Because I have a good relationship with my dad?"

"You care. Too many people who have been through

what you have would harden their soul against letting in any kind of softer feelings, but you haven't. You care about your father, you cared about Jim the other day on the beach, you care about our patients and about your refugee patients thousands of miles away."

She had to kiss him. Though she knew it was potentially dangerous, she couldn't resist rising on her tiptoes and pressing her mouth to his.

He remained frozen for one breathless moment, and then he lowered his mouth to hers and kissed her as she realized both of them had been craving all night.

It was raw and hot, his mouth searching hers, his body pressed against her. She realized as his arms tightened around her that she had been fooling herself. She hadn't kissed him out of tenderness or empathy but because she had been craving his kiss since those magical moments the day before, outside the beach gate.

She made a soft sound and wrapped her arms around his neck, her mouth angled to allow him better access. Her breasts ached where they were pressed against him. *Everything* ached.

His mouth was urgent and demanding on hers, and the hunger in it aroused her.

He wanted her.

She didn't need to feel the hard nudge of his arousal against her to sense it in his hands and his mouth and his body. They were alone in the house. She could take him by the hand and tug him into her bedroom, and they could spend the rest of this rainy, misty night wrapped together, pushing away the shadows.

The temptation consumed her. How easy it would be

to take that step. It had been so very long since she had felt wanted and needed and cherished like this.

And then what? If she and Eli spent the night together, where would that leave them? He was still committed to leaving. He had just told her all his reasons for it. He was driven to continue the work he had been doing, providing medical care to people in need. She understood now that he was motivated by a complicated tangle of guilt and grief and obligation. She also understood that she would be a fool to think she would be enough to keep him here.

Her heart would be broken. Just like her marriage—which she had known even as she was saying *I do* was a mistake that never should have happened—it would be her own stupid fault.

One the best ways she had found to discipline Skye on the rare occasions her daughter misbehaved was to redirect, to encourage her to make a better choice. Those words, *make a better choice*, were often all she needed to say when Skye was throwing one of her rare tantrums or doing something Melissa had told her not to do.

She needed to listen to her own advice to her daughter. She had no hope of creating happiness in life if she made choices she knew from the outset would only lead to heartbreak and pain.

She couldn't make love with him, as much as she ached to feel his arms around her all night long, to learn all his secrets and explore that delicious body.

It would leave her too vulnerable. She was already half in love with the man. Spending what was left of the night together would push her headlong the rest of the way.

She had entrusted her heart and her life to one man who put something else ahead of her. Fixing her mistake had cost her dearly, and her child would pay the price for that the rest of her life, forever separated from one parent or the other through the tangled maze of custody and visitations.

She couldn't wander blindly into a similar situation. When he walked away to return to the military and the life that gave him such purpose and meaning, Melissa was very much afraid she would never put back together the pieces of her shattered heart.

She didn't want to end the kiss. She wanted to stay right here forever, with his warm, sexy mouth teasing out all her secrets. Just a few more moments…

He was finally the one who broke the embrace. He eased his mouth away and rested his forehead against hers.

She thought she smelled roses again, but this time the scent was wistful and almost sad.

"Didn't we say we weren't going to do this again?" he said, his forehead pressed to hers.

She wanted to make some smart response but couldn't think of anything. "Kisses don't count in the middle of the night."

"I think that's when they count the most."

After a moment, he stepped away, eyes haunted with regret. "I need to go, before I forget all the reasons why I can't stay."

Her chest ached and she wished with all her heart that things could be different, that she could be the woman for him.

"What about Max?" he asked.

Already the house seemed to echo with emptiness. For all that the ghosts of Brambleberry House seemed friendly enough, she wasn't sure she was strong enough to face them alone tonight. "He's here and he seems comfortable enough. If you don't mind, I'll keep him overnight."

"No problem."

He looked as if he had other things he wanted to say, but Eli finally headed for the door. When he opened it, Melissa saw the light rain of earlier had turned into a steady downpour. It matched her sudden mood—dank, dark, dismal.

"Good night," he said with one last, backward look that seemed filled with regret.

Was he regretting that he had to leave?

Or regretting that they both knew he couldn't stay?

After he walked out into the night, Melissa locked the door behind him, then went through her apartment turning off lights, grateful for Max's company as he followed along behind her.

Her heart ached as she thought of the story Eli had told and the sadness behind it. He must have cared about the woman very much to shoulder such a burden six months later. This Justine person must have been remarkable. Not the kind of woman who basically fell apart simply because her daughter was spending the night with her father.

She had learned to be tough after the divorce, and she needed to call on that strength. Something told her she would need all the courage she could find after Eli left Cannon Beach once more.

Chapter Nine

The next day, Sunday, she rose early despite her late night and took Max for a run along the beach. He didn't have Fiona's loping grade but toddled along beside her so cheerfully, it warmed her heart.

The day had turned cooler from the rain of the night before, with more precipitation predicted for later that evening. April could be fickle on the coast, with the rare warm, pleasant day often giving way to a spring snowstorm.

Things weren't supposed to be that drastic, but it was definitely cold enough first thing in the morning that she was grateful for her jacket.

They didn't bump into Eli, as she had half hoped and half feared. All in all, it was the most uneventful run she'd had on the beach in what felt like forever.

As if to remind her of previous fun times, her wrist ached more than it had in days as she and Max returned to the house. She ignored it and spent the rest of the morning trying not to watch the clock as she finished some of her coursework for her online nurse practitioner classes.

She had just hit Send on another assignment when Max suddenly scampered to the front door just moments before it opened.

"Mommy! Hi! Where are you, Mommy?"

She hurried out to the entryway to find Skye and Cody standing just inside the door. Skye must have used her key to come in.

"You're back! Hi, honey."

"Hi, Mommy." Skye hugged her but didn't stop frowning. "Hey, why do you have Dr. Sanderson's dog? Hi, Max!"

"He's babysitting me," she said. Skye giggled while Cody looked on, confused.

She didn't bother to explain to him. "How did things go?" she asked instead.

She didn't necessarily want Skye to rant about how miserable she'd been overnight. Melissa didn't want to think she was that small-minded.

Still, when her daughter beamed, Melissa had to smile through clenched teeth.

"So fun," Skye said. "We went to a baseball game last night and they had fireworks and everything. Then we had pizza and this morning we went to the store. We were going to go to another baseball game but decided not to. I got to see Grandma and Grandpa Fielding, too. Did you know they have a swimming pool at their new house?"

Her in-laws had only recently moved to Portland from Manzanita and she hadn't been to their house yet.

"I didn't know that. How fun."

Skye made a face. "Dad said it was too cold to go swimming, plus I didn't take my suit."

"Next time, though," Cody promised.

"Do we want to set up the next visit?" she asked her ex.

Cody looked a little distracted, as if he hadn't thought past this one. "I don't know what my schedule's going to look like next week. We might be heading down to Cali. What about two weeks from now?"

She forced a smile. "That could work. Just let me know."

"Thanks, Missy. Hey, Skye-ster. Thanks for hanging with me. I've got to run."

"Okay. Bye, Dad."

"Sorry to leave so fast. Amalia didn't do well on the drive here. She's a bit carsick so I'd better get her back to the city."

"No problem. Next time I could meet you halfway."

"That would be great. You're the best, Miss. Thanks!"

She waved him off, proud of herself for taking the high road this time. It made things go so much more smoothly when she tried to be the adult in their interactions.

After he hurried down the steps, she smiled at her daughter, who was busy petting Max.

"Why is he really here?"

"I wanted some company last night. The house was pretty empty since everyone but me was gone for the night."

"Even Fiona?"

"She went with Rosa on a hiking trip out of town. So, yes, it was just me."

"We should get our own dog."

It was not a new request. Skye had been pushing for their own dog since they had moved from Hawaii.

"Maybe when we get into our own house. I'm so glad you had a great time with your father and Amalia. Is she nice?"

"Really nice. She doesn't say much, but she's trying to learn English. She taught me a little Portuguese. That's what they speak in Brazil, not Brazilian, did you know that?"

"That I did know."

"I don't know why. It's weird, if you ask me. But she taught me how to say hello—*olá*, which kind of sounds like *hola*. And goodbye is *adeus*, which also sounds like *adios*. Thank you is *obrigada*. Dad would say *obrigado* but I'm not sure why. It was fun, except I missed you a ton. Maybe you could come next time."

Wouldn't that be delightful? She swallowed a groan and chose her words carefully. "That's sweet of you, honey, but it's important for you to enjoy your special time with your dad and new stepmom. And soon you'll have a new baby brother to love. You get plenty of time with me."

"I guess. I still missed you."

"I missed you, too. So much, I had to borrow Max here to keep me company."

"I wish we didn't have to give him back."

"I know, honey. But you like sleeping in your own bed and I'm sure Max does, too."

"I guess."

Melissa didn't want to fall into the trap of trying to compete with her ex for most fun parent, but she'd been without her daughter for an entire day and wanted to have a little fun with her while she could. "Why don't you go get your kite and we can take Max home, then fly your kite on that good stretch of beach by Dr. Sanderson's house."

Skye had been begging her to take the kite out for several weeks and she latched onto the idea with enthusiasm. "Yay! I'll go get it."

She skipped to her room, leaving Melissa to gather up the dog's things and try not to be nervous at the idea of seeing Eli again.

As he finished putting together the lift recliner he had purchased that morning, Eli wasn't sure whether his father would be happy about the gift or would accuse him of trying to turn Wendell into an old man before his time.

His father was recovering from a double knee replacement. Nobody would think less of him for using anything that might make his life a little more comfortable. And after all his father did for his patients around town, didn't he deserve a comfortable chair at the end of the day that he could get into and out of without pain?

It was a good argument, if Eli did say so himself.

Whether his father would buy into it was another story entirely.

He pulled the chair into the corner where his father's beat-up old recliner held pride of place. He would never dare to get rid of the thing, but he could at least offer this one as an alternative. If nothing else, Max would probably like it.

He looked around automatically for the dog, then remembered. Max had spent the night with Melissa.

Lucky dog.

He pushed the dangerous thought away as he settled into the recliner to check it out. He couldn't think about her like that.

How had she made it through the night? It had taken all his strength that morning not to walk up to Brambleberry House to check on her.

That hadn't stopped him from thinking about her all day. Their hot, intense kiss had haunted him, kept him awake most of the night.

What was he going to do about this attraction to her?

Absolutely nothing.

What could come of it? She deserved better than a long-distance relationship, and that was all he could offer her right now. He was leaving town as soon as his father was back on his legs. Eli had had an email just that morning from his commanding officer, asking when he would be back and whether he was ready to take off again to return to his job overseas.

For one crazy moment, Eli had been tempted to tell Dr. Flores that he was done, he wasn't going to re-up but would continue serving the National Guard, available when his country needed him.

He knew the woman would be disappointed but wouldn't think less of him. Many—in fact, most—army doctors didn't stay in as long as he had, at least not on active duty. His initial commitment had only been two years, but the work had been so fulfilling he hadn't been able to walk away then.

Could he walk away now? That was the million-dollar question. Before Justine and Miri died, he had been thinking about going into private practice while retaining his military benefits by serving in the Guard. That was the course most in the Army Medical Corps eventually took.

Since that horrible day in that dusty market town, he had felt driven to do more, try harder, dedicate himself more fully.

He owed both of them. Didn't he? He hadn't been able to save Justine, but he could help those she had cared about.

That left little place in his world for someone like Melissa, who had finally found her own place to belong here in Cannon Beach.

While he might accept that intellectually, it hadn't stopped him from thinking about her all day, remembering their kiss and feeling comforted all over again when he remembered the sweet way she had wrapped her arms around him in her kitchen, offering solace and concern.

He had it bad for Melissa Fielding. That was the plain truth. He was all tangled up over her and didn't know how to unravel the silken cords around his heart.

The doorbell startled him out of his thoughts, and it took him a minute to figure out how to work the control of the chair enough to put the footrest down so he could get out.

When he opened the door, he was greeted first by a familiar woof, and then by a grin and wave from a young curly-haired girl.

“Hi, the other Dr. Sanderson.”

He was as charmed by Skye as he was by her mother, even though her bright smile reminded him so painfully of Miri. “Hi there, the other Ms. Fielding.”

She grinned. “Mom said we had to take Max back to you today, even though I really, really, really wanted to keep him.”

He glanced at Skye’s mother and felt that peculiar tug in his gut that had also become familiar since he’d come back to town, the one he felt only around Melissa. He wanted to tell the girl she could keep the dog for another night, but he had a feeling Melissa would not appreciate his offer.

“Thank you. Both of you.”

“Thanks for loaning him,” Melissa said. “He was wonderful company, weren’t you, Max?”

The dog yipped as if agreeing with her.

“Here’s his stuff.” Skye handed over the bowls and blanket he had taken to Brambleberry House the night before.

“Thanks.” He took them and set them inside his father’s house, then gestured to the colorful fabric kite in Melissa’s hand. “I guess I can tell where you guys are going after this.”

"Yep," Skye answered. "I've been begging and begging to fly our kite and today Mom said yes. We're going down to the beach by your house because the wind is always just right."

"Looks like a great kite."

It was shaped like a jellyfish, purple with rainbow-colored tentacles. "You should see how high it goes. Sometimes it goes up and up until I can barely even see it."

"Sounds amazing."

He and his mom used to fly kites on the beach often after school. It had been one of their favorite pastimes. After the cancer made her too weak, she used to sit at the window here and watch him down on the beach below their house. Some nights he would fly a kite past dusk, hesitant to come in when he knew she enjoyed the sight of it flying and dipping so much.

"You can come with us," Skye suggested. "We always have a hard time getting it up in the air. I can never run fast enough to have the wind take it. Maybe you could help us."

He darted a look at Melissa but couldn't tell by her veiled expression what she thought about her daughter's spontaneous invitation.

"It's been a long time since I've flown a kite. I'm not sure I remember how."

"We can show you," Skye said.

"I'm sure Dr. Sanderson has other things to do right now," Melissa said.

"Like what?" Skye asked.

"Skye. It's rude to expect him to drop everything and come with us."

He ought to let the girl down gently and tell her he had other plans. But suddenly he wanted to fly a kite more than he had wanted to do anything else in a long time…except, perhaps, to kiss her mother.

"Thank you for inviting me," he said instead. "I would very much enjoy helping you fly this beautiful kite."

It definitely wasn't a good idea to spend more time with Melissa or with her daughter, not when he was having a hard time resisting both of them, but he told himself he could handle it. He only had to keep things in perspective, remind himself he was leaving in a few weeks.

He couldn't tell how Melissa felt about the prospect of him coming along, but her daughter made her delight clear. She beamed at him, the gap in her front teeth more pronounced. "Yay! Can Max come with us?"

"Sure. I don't see why not."

"I'll hold his leash, if you want."

"Thanks," he said, trying to keep the dryness out of his tone. "That's very nice of you."

He picked up his sunglasses from the hall table where he'd left them and walked outside into a lovely Oregon afternoon. The rain of the evening before was nowhere in evidence, though he knew the forecast called for possible heavy waves and wind later in the week.

"Let me take that," he said to Melissa, reaching for the colorful kite she carried.

"It's a kite. It's not exactly heavy."

"If it were heavy, it wouldn't fly," Skye pointed out with irrefutable logic.

"It's big and bulky, though. I don't mind."

She held it out for him. "Here you go. Knock yourself out."

He reached for it and though he didn't plan to and, in fact, actively tried to avoid it, his hands brushed hers.

Heat seemed to race along his nerve endings and his stomach muscles clenched.

So much for keeping control around her. If he could have that kind of reaction from a little accidental slide of skin on skin, he was in big trouble.

As they took the closest beach access, a narrow trail between two houses, Skye hurried ahead of them with Max, leaving Eli to walk alone with Melissa.

"You really didn't have to come with us," she said after a moment. "Skye is right, we're not the greatest at getting the kite up in the air, but trying is half the fun."

Her cheeks were pink, but he couldn't tell if that was from embarrassment or from the breeze.

"I meant what I said. I'm looking forward to it. What better way to spend a windy April afternoon?"

When they reached the beach, she gave him a sidelong look.

"All morning, I've been thinking about how awkward it would be to face you again," she admitted, confirming his suspicion about the source of that rosy glow. "I'm kind of glad we got that out of the way now, instead of tomorrow morning in the office when you're seeing a patient."

Her words were a blunt reminder that she worked for

his father. He had a strong suspicion that wasn't accidental, as if she needed both of them to remember their respective roles.

"You have nothing to feel awkward or embarrassed about," he assured her.

She snorted. "Sure. I only drank too much, which I never do, fell asleep in your car and then practically dragged you into my house and insisted on feeding you." She glanced at her daughter and then back at him. "And it's my fault we kissed again, when we both made it clear the first time that it shouldn't happen again."

Was she sorry it had happened? He couldn't tell from her response. He wasn't sure he regretted it. He should, he knew, but her kiss had been as warm and nurturing as the rest of her.

He wanted to kiss her again. Right now, right here. Instead, he gripped the kite more tightly and continued walking beside her while the April breeze that smelled of sand and sea danced around them. "It was a strange night. We're going to chalk it all up to that, right?"

She opened her mouth as if to argue, but her daughter interrupted before she could.

"What about here?" Skye asked. "Is this a good place to fly a kite?"

He managed to drag his gaze away from Melissa's mouth to focus on their surroundings, the beach a short distance from his father's house. "This looks like an excellent spot. No trees, no wires, no skyscrapers."

"I agree. It's a great place," Melissa said. She set her backpack on the sand and reached inside, pulling out a rolled sand mat. After spreading it out, she plopped down, then calmly pulled a book out of the backpack.

"I do believe this is a great spot for me to sit back and relax with a book while you guys run around and get all sweaty trying to get that big kite up in the air. I'll watch our stuff."

Eli snorted. "You're going to read a book while I help your daughter fly her kite. Why do I get the feeling I've just been played?"

She shrugged nonchalantly. "Nobody is playing anybody. If you remember correctly, I had no idea you would be here. We were only supposed to be dropping Max off at your place before coming down to fly the kite. I didn't plan things this way, but since you're here, I would be crazy to waste a chance to sit on the sand and enjoy this warm afternoon."

He laughed, completely delighted with her. Every time he was with her, he fell harder.

She stared at him, her features still and watchful, with an expression he couldn't read behind her sunglasses.

I wish you would do that more often. I like it so much.

He remembered her slightly tipsy words the night before in his dad's SUV after he had laughed then, and his insides felt achy with need. That encounter seemed a hundred miles away right now on this sunny beach with the waves washing against the sand and the seagulls crying out overhead.

After a moment, he turned to Skye. "Your mom wants to read her book and I can't argue it's a good plan. I guess it's up to us to fly this kite, then."

"We can do it," Skye said again. She jutted her chin into the air, looking like a mini pugilist version of her mother. "I know we can."

"You got it. Let's do this."

The afternoon turned into one of the most enjoyable he had spent in a long time.

He tried to steel his heart against Skye, using as a shield an image of a little dark-eyed orphan with a shy smile, but he quickly realized it was pointless.

He couldn't resist her any more than he'd been able to resist her mother.

Skye was completely adorable. She chattered endlessly about everything under the sun. She told him about the haystacks, how they had been formed by wind and water eons ago. She waved energetically at the people on recumbent bicycles who rode past them with some frequency on the hard-packed sand close to the water, telling him about the time she and her mother had rented them once when they first moved back to town and it had been really fun. She talked about her father and his new wife and the baby on the way and how it was a boy and she couldn't wait to hold him.

She was smart and funny and as openhearted as her mother.

Max ran around in excitement as they worked to get the kite up. Once it was soaring and dipping above them on the currents, the dog seemed to lose interest and plopped down beside Melissa, who reached absently to pet him while turning the page of her book with her other hand.

Whenever he looked over at her, his chest seemed to ache all over again. The sunlight gleamed in her hair and she looked fresh and sweet and beautiful.

It was a perfect moment here, beside the water he loved. A girl laughing with glee, her mother soft and relaxed on the sand, the wind catching the colorful kite and tugging it ever higher.

The restlessness inside him seemed to settle for now, and he wanted the moment to go on and on.

He and Skye flew the kite for over an hour, taking turns holding it and letting it dip and dance on the currents.

He thought Melissa might have fallen asleep, but he couldn't tell for sure with her sunglasses.

Sometime later, she finally rose with her elegant grace and came over to where he and Skye were holding the kite. "You guys have done a great job."

"It's higher than we've ever got it!" Skye exclaimed. "Eli is the *best* at flying a kite. He said he used to do it with his mom when he was a kid and flying a kite always makes him think of her."

Melissa sent him a swift look, and Eli pointedly busied himself with the kite.

"We should probably go, kiddo. We still have to fix dinner and get you to bed."

"Oh. Do we have to?"

"I'm afraid so. You had a big weekend with your dad. You don't want to be too tired for school tomorrow, right? It's your big field trip."

"Oh, yeah!" To Eli, she said, "We're going to the lighthouse in Astoria and my teacher said we could maybe even fly paper airplanes off the top of it. We're going to write our names on them and see whose goes the farthest. I bet it will be mine."

He remembered flying paper airplanes off that lighthouse when he was in elementary school and still remembered the triumph of his particular design beating everyone else in his class. "Sounds like fun. You'll have to let me know if you're the winner."

"I will."

Together, they started the process of winding the string from the kite back onto the reel. The kite fought them on the currents until he was able to pull it back down to earth.

"What do you say to Eli?" her mother prompted once they had the colorful kite back on the sand.

"Thanks a ton for helping me, Eli."

Skye beamed at him. Before he realized what she intended, she threw her arms around his waist and gave him a tight hug.

Emotions came out of nowhere and clogged his throat, much to his embarrassment, his mind on another girl who would never have the chance to fly kites on a beautiful April afternoon.

"It was my pleasure. Truly."

"I hope we can do it again sometime."

He didn't know how to answer. He would be gone again soon. Even if his father wasn't yet up to full strength, Eli would have to go and let a substitute doctor take his place. "Maybe."

"And you said I could play pool at your dad's house. Can we do that tonight?"

"No," Melissa said firmly. "Maybe another time."

He regretted that he likely wouldn't have the chance to follow through on his offer to let her come over and practice before he left town. Maybe his father could take on billiards lessons while he was recovering from his knee surgery. He would suggest it to Wendell the next day when he went to his father's rehabilitation center.

"I'll walk you back," he said after Melissa had gathered up her things.

"You don't have to do that."

"Somebody needs to haul this guy back for you."

She didn't argue, but he could tell she didn't need or want his help.

He couldn't tell her he would find any excuse to spend more time with her, already dreading the moment he would have to say goodbye.

As she walked along beside him, with Skye again racing ahead of them holding tight to Max's leash, Melissa came to the grave realization that she didn't need to worry any more that she might do something stupid like fall in love with Eli.

She already had.

Watching him fly a kite with Skye, seeing his patience and his kindness and the sheer fun he seemed to have with her daughter, had made that truth abundantly clear.

How could any woman hope to resist him? He was sexy and sweet and wonderful.

What a complete disaster. He was going to leave again. What was she supposed to do then?

When they reached Brambleberry House, he opened the sea gate for her. She was relieved when she spotted Fiona, who immediately rushed across the lawn to greet Max, tail wagging.

"Looks like your neighbor is back."

She waved to Rosa, who was sitting on the swing looking out at the water.

Rosa waved back, and Melissa didn't need to see her expression to guess she was wearing a speculative look seeing her with Eli again.

Rosa could speculate all she wanted. They were only together temporarily. He would be leaving soon and she would be alone again.

"Thanks for letting me fly the kite with you," he said to Skye. "I had a great time."

"Thanks again for helping me. Me and my mom never would've been able to get it up that high."

"I don't know. You seem like a pro."

"Thanks." She beamed at him. "Now that you showed me what to do, I bet the next time I can get it as high as you did this time."

"I don't doubt it for a minute."

"You can come watch and tell me if I'm doing it right," she declared.

"Maybe."

He wouldn't be here. He would be off saving the world, leaving them here to figure out how to fly kites and play billiards without him. Melissa frowned but didn't want to ruin her daughter's happiness by pointing out that depressing truth.

"I guess I'll see you at the office tomorrow," she said instead.

"Right. I guess so."

With other friends, she might have hugged them or even given a kiss on the cheek before sending them on their way. With all these emotions churning through her, she didn't dare do anything but give Eli an awkward little wave.

He looked as if he wanted to say something else, but he finally nodded and waved, gripped Max's leash and headed back down the beach.

She did her best not to watch after him, though it took every ounce of self-control she had.

"I am so ready to have this baby, if only to be done with stirrups and paper gowns."

Melissa smiled at Julia Garrett, currently settled onto the exam table in said paper gown. "It looks so lovely on you. Are you sure you don't want a few more children?"

Julia made a face. "No. This is it. Our house is bursting at the seams and Will says he can't build on again and I can't bear to move. So we have to be done."

"At least until Maddie and Simon go off to college next year. Then you'll have plenty of room for more babies."

She gave a rough laugh. "I hope you hear how ridiculous that sounds. We'll never be empty nesters at this rate."

This was Julia's fifth child. She and her husband, Will, had her teenage twin boy and girl from her previous marriage as well as an eight-year-old and a four-year-old. Melissa could only imagine the chaos at their house, but Julia always seemed calm and composed. Oh, how she envied her and wished some of that serenity would rub off on her.

Julia had once lived in Brambleberry House with her twins, when she was a single widow with twins, before she married Will. She had a soft spot for the house and the gardens and the stunning beauty of the place.

When Melissa came back to town, the two of them had bonded over that right after they met, a bond that had deepened and strengthened into real friendship in the months since.

"This is the last one, for sure."

She touched her abdomen protectively and Melissa felt a sharp little ache in her own womb.

She had wanted more children but hadn't been willing to bring more children into the uncertainty of a shaky marriage.

The little twinge of regret annoyed her. She had an amazing daughter. She refused to waste the wonderful life she had, wishing she had made different choices.

"Dr. Sanderson should be here soon."

"When you say that, I keep picturing sweet Dr. Sanderson, then remember you're talking about someone else entirely. How is it, working for Wendell's son? He's quite gorgeous, isn't he?"

Oh, yes. Entirely *too* gorgeous. She had to brace herself against her instinctive reaction to him every time she came into the office. It had been three weeks since he came back to town, two since the day he had come with her and Skye to fly kites, and she was more tangled up than ever.

"Just like his father, Eli is an excellent doctor," she said. "I promise you'll be in great hands."

"Oh, I know. He was great when I came in for my checkup last week and the week before. Wendell has nothing but praise for him. Will remembers him, though Eli is a few years younger. Will said he was freaky smart in school."

Julia hadn't grown up in Cannon Beach but had spent summers here during her childhood. Will had been her first love, which Melissa found utterly charming.

"He was," she answered, wondering how they'd gotten on the subject of Eli. She had been doing her best *not* to think about him…which was particularly tough when they worked together each day. The only way she had survived the last few weeks was by staying busy with her classes and Skye and trying not to think about him leaving.

"How soon before his dad is back?"

"We're still not sure. His own doctors want him to take it easy, but you know Wendell. He is determined to come in next week for at least a few hours a day. Who knows, he might be back before you have the baby. When are you due again?"

"Three more weeks."

"Your chances are good, then."

She was aware with every passing day that Eli's time in Cannon Beach was drawing to a close. The prospect of him leaving filled her with a curious mix of dread and relief. She dreaded knowing he would be gone and she would be left to worry about him possibly being in harm's way. But she couldn't deny there would be a certain relief that she wouldn't have to pretend any more that she wasn't crazy in love with the man.

She had done her best to keep things polite and professional between them. She helped him in exams, she did triage assessment, she answered phone calls and forwarded prescriptions to him. And every time she was with him, she was aware of her feelings growing stronger by the moment.

He was an excellent doctor, compassionate and kind, as well as a devoted, loving son. She was head over heels and already aching at the idea that he wouldn't be in her life every day.

She pushed away the worry to focus on their patient. "Do you want Eli to wait a few minutes before doing your checkup, until Will can get here?"

"Better not. He wasn't sure if he would make it back to town in time. He's on a job up in Seaside, doing a bathroom remodel for a lady."

Her husband was a master carpenter who had done some amazing work at Brambleberry House and other places around town.

"I'll let Eli know you're ready, then."

When she opened the door, she found him pulling the chart out of the polished wood holder beside the door, which, she remembered now, Will Garrett had built right around the time she started working for Wendell Sanderson.

"Julia is ready when you are."

"Thanks." He gave her the same kind of careful smile

they had both become experts at over the last few weeks. She had a feeling he felt as awkward and uncertain around her as she did around him.

He entered the exam room and she followed behind as he shook Julia's hand with a warm, comforting smile that made Melissa's ovaries tingle. Darn them.

"How are you feeling? Things are probably getting tight in there."

"Any tighter and I'm afraid I'm going to bust through the seams."

"Let's just take a look at things."

He listened to the baby's heartbeat first, then did a quick exam with brisk professionalism.

"Looks like you're only dilated to a one, so I think it's safe to say we still have a few weeks to go."

Melissa adjusted the sheet over her and then helped her sit up.

"The twins were a week early," Julia said, "but Tess was born the day before her due date and her brother was born the day after his."

Eli said. "You're the expert after five of these. I'm sure you can tell me a thousand ways every pregnancy is different, but it's good to know the pattern."

"No offense, Dr. Sanderson, but I was telling Melissa I would love it if your dad was back in action by the time I deliver. You've been great, but he delivered Will as well as my younger two kids and he's become kind of part of the family."

"None taken," Eli assured her. "I wish I had an answer for you. He's coming in for a few hours a day next week, though his surgeon and physical therapist want him to take it easy. Maybe he'll be back just in time to deliver your little girl."

"I hope so. He's home, right?"

"Yes. He came home a few weeks ago."

The day after they had flown kites and walked with Max along the beach, in fact, after rebounding quickly from the temporary setback of his tumble. Melissa had been by to see him twice on her lunch hour and once with Skye after school. All three times she had managed to miss Eli.

"How is he doing?" Julia asked.

"Bored out of his mind," Eli said with a smile. "My dad is the kind of guy who likes to be on the go. I knew the toughest part of his recovery would be the monotony of being sidelined. But his knees are already stronger than they've been in years, so the surgery was a good thing, for him and for his patients here in Cannon Beach."

He wrapped up the appointment a few moments later with another handshake and a warm smile.

After he left, Julia shook her head at Melissa. "I love Dr. Sanderson Sr., I'm not going to lie, but that son of his. Yum. Honestly, even though I'm extremely pregnant and extremely happily married, I don't know how you keep from constantly melting into a pile of hormones with that slow smile of his."

Melissa couldn't tell her friend she did exactly that. "He's my boss," she reminded Julia. "I have to keep my hormones—and everything else—to myself where he's concerned."

"Good luck with that," Julia said with a laugh.

Melissa forced a smile. She needed far more than luck where Eli was concerned.

Eli wasn't sure what had happened, but somehow over the last few weeks, since the Sunday afternoon when he had gone with her and Skye to fly the girl's kite, Melissa had withdrawn from him, treating him with a polite reserve that was far different from the friendship that had been growing between them.

She wasn't rude. In fact, she was respectful and professional, but as distant as if he were just some scrub who had stepped in to help out at his dad's practice in Wendell's absence.

He was glad, he told himself. He had crossed too many lines he shouldn't have with her.

Still, he missed her easy smiles and her funny sense of humor and the warmth that seemed to envelop him around her.

"You all know my dad wants to come in next week," he said to her, Carmen and Tiffany as the three women prepared to leave for the day on Friday.

"I hope he doesn't overdo," Carmen said with her characteristic frown. "My sister had knee replacement surgery and had to have the whole thing done all over again six months later."

"We'll all have to make sure he takes it easy. It's going to have to be a team effort. But the truth is, he's going crazy at home after three weeks away and thinks his patients need him. He won't be up for much patient care, but he should be fine handling consultations or refilling prescriptions, if he could do that from his desk. We'll all have to watch out for him."

"We can make sure he behaves," Tiffany said. "I'm glad he's coming in. I was hoping he'd be back before I leave."

The CNA had put in her notice the week before and had been talking nonstop about her plans to move to Los Angeles, where they already had a manager and a few gigs lined up.

"It will be good to have him back," Melissa said. "I've missed him."

"I'll add a few appointments into his schedule," Carmen said. "Nothing too drastic. Just consultations, like you said."

"He wants to jump back into things with both of his artificial knees, but I worry about him overdoing."

"Sounds good, especially since you're going to be leaving us soon," Carmen said.

Against his will, he glanced at Melissa. Had she stiffened at that?

"Yes. I'll be here until the end of next week, and then I have to report to duty again. I've already talked to the medical temp agency in Portland about sending a replacement until my dad is back up to speed."

"We'll miss you," Carmen said gruffly.

"Especially the female patients," Tiffany said with a teasing grin.

Eli could feel his face flush and he forced himself not to look at Melissa, who hadn't said a word.

"If that's everything, can I go?" Tiffany asked. "We're

playing down in Manzanita tonight, at least until the power goes out from the big storm on the way."

"They're not canceling your gig?" Melissa finally asked.

Tiffany shook her head. "Not that I've heard. The storm's not supposed to be here until nine or so. We'll play until we can't play anymore."

"That's the spirit," Carmen said.

"Could be nobody else will show up, then we can all go home. So can I take off?"

"Yes. That's all," Eli said. "I just wanted to talk for a moment about the plan next week for my dad's return. Good luck with your show."

She flashed him a grin as she grabbed her backpack and hurried out the door, humming some of the lyrics he recognized from the night he and Melissa had gone to see her.

"I'm off, too," Carmen said. "I have to head to the grocery store. Every time the wind blows around here, the grocery stores run out of milk."

She hurried off after Tiffany. For the first time in longer than he could remember, he and Melissa were alone.

She jumped up from her desk and grabbed her sweater and her purse. "I need to go, too," Melissa said.

No, he wasn't imagining things. She was doing her utmost to avoid his company. He knew it was for the best so they didn't cross any more lines, but he missed her with a fierce ache.

"Big weekend plans?"

She made a face. "Cody's coming to pick Skye up again tonight. He wants to have her the whole weekend until Sunday this time, so I need to help her pack. He wants to get out of town before the storm hits. I tried to convince him it wasn't a good weekend for his visitation, but he insisted since he's going to be busy next weekend. Also, his sister is in town and she hasn't seen Skye in about a year."

"Go take care of what you need to at home. Don't worry about things here. I'll lock up."

"Thank you."

She gave him a stiff nod, gathered her purse from under her desk and hurried for the door.

That was the most personal conversation they had shared in days. He felt an ache, missing the warm, funny woman he had come to know since returning to Cannon Beach.

It was better this way, that she had put up these walls between them, but he felt an ache.

How had she reacted when he'd said he would only be there another week? He hadn't been able to read her. Had she been relieved? Or would she miss him as deeply as he knew he would miss her?

He rubbed at that ache in his chest. Somehow Melissa had worked her way inside his own careful walls. She was there, lodged against his heart, and he didn't know how he was going to push her out again.

Chapter Ten

The storm hit about four hours after Cody left for Portland with Skye in his impractical sports car.

Melissa sat in the window seat in the sunroom she loved, watching the waves grow higher as the sky darkened with rolling clouds.

Storms always made her blood hum. One good thing about formerly being married to a professional surfer—they had always lived next to an ocean. Whether it was Mexico or Hawaii or Australia, no matter what coastal area she and Cody and Skye had been living, she had always loved watching storms hit land, as long as she could observe the drama from somewhere safe.

She wasn't as crazy about being in the middle of them. She had been, a few times. Once she had been working at a hospital in Maui in the midst of a Category

3 hurricane and had worked for thirty-six hours straight when her coworkers couldn't make it to the hospital because of the storm.

Skye loved storms. She would have loved this one. Her daughter would have found it a great adventure to cuddle together and tell stories by candlelight. She missed her with a deep ache, which she knew was perfectly ridiculous. Somehow Melissa had to get used to these weekends without her child. She wanted her daughter to have a relationship with her father, and Skye and Cody couldn't truly have that through only occasional phone calls and video chats.

Melissa had lost her father when she was fourteen and still felt the emptiness of that. She didn't want Skye to grow up being resentful or angry that Cody wasn't in her life. Somehow she had to come to terms with being without her and fill the void with friends and hobbies.

The power went out two hours later, as she expected. Through the window, she could see only darkness, which told her Brambleberry House wasn't the only structure hit. It appeared power was out up and down the coast.

Fortunately, her e-reader was fully charged and would last for hours, and she had already gathered all the emergency supplies she might need during a storm.

She wasn't looking forward to a long night alone in the dark, but she tried to make her situation as comfortable as possible, lighting candles she had gathered earlier and carrying pillows and blankets to the window seat.

If the winds increased in intensity, she would probably feel safer away from the windows and the possibility of shattering glass from flying tree limbs or other debris, but for now she didn't feel in harm's way.

She was just settling in with her book when she heard a knock at the door.

"It's Rosa," she heard from outside. "And Fiona."

Melissa hurried to the door and found her friend standing in the entry holding two lit candles, her Irish setter at her side.

"This is some kind of storm, no?"

"It's crazy out there."

"Did I see our Skye go off with her father earlier tonight? Did they make it all right?"

She nodded, warmed by Rosa's use of the possessive pronoun when it came to her daughter. She loved having friends who cared. This was the reason she had come back to Cannon Beach, to forge this kind of powerful connection.

"He texted me that they were safely back in Portland and it wasn't even raining there."

"That's a relief." Rosa looked inside the apartment, where Melissa had lit a couple of emergency candles to push away the darkness. "I came down to check on you and make sure you had some kind of flashlight or candle, but it looks like you are all set."

This wasn't her first spring storm along the coast. Sometimes the big ones could wipe out power in the region for days.

"I should be fine. Thank you for worrying about me. Have you checked on Sonia?"

Rosa nodded, looking worried. "I know she doesn't like storms much."

Though it was nothing the other woman had told her, Melissa had the same impression during the most recent storm. Sonia became even more brusque than normal, her words clipped, and Melissa thought she glimpsed fear layering beneath it.

"I checked on her first. She assured me she is fine, that she has plenty of LED candles. She had four or five going, with extra batteries if necessary, so they can go all night, if it comes to that."

"I hope it doesn't." Again, she wondered about Sonia and the mysterious past that left her afraid of the dark.

"Since Skye is not here, do you want me to leave Fiona with you for the company? I asked Sonia and she said she would be fine."

Poor Rosa, having to watch over everyone in Brambleberry House. It wasn't her job, but somehow they all had become her responsibility anyway.

She patted Fiona, wishing she could say yes. She never would have guessed she would find so much solace in canine companionship. She and Skye really needed to get serious about going to the shelter and picking out a rescue.

"That's so sweet of you, but I think I'm okay. Much better than last time Skye was with her dad."

Rosa gave her a sympathetic look. "I'm sorry. Being a mother is hard business, no? It never seems to become easier."

That seemed an odd statement, filled with more knowledge than she might have expected from a woman who didn't have any children, at least as far as Melissa knew. Maybe it was just Rosa's unique word choices, where English was her second language.

She couldn't deny the truth in what her friend said, though. "It's so hard," she agreed.

"If you want some chocolate and the sympathy, you know where to find me. I can maybe find a bottle of wine somewhere, also. We don't need light for that."

She managed a smile, tempted for a moment by the picture Rosa painted. Wine and chocolate and sympathy might just be the perfect prescription during a storm.

On the other hand, she wouldn't be good company for anyone.

This time, she knew her dark mood was only partially about the pang she felt at being separated from her child. The rest was about Eli and this wild morass of emotions she didn't know what to do about.

He would be there another week, he had said that afternoon. She had nearly gasped aloud at his words as the shock of them had ripped through her like a sharp blade. She was still trying to process the idea that she only had one more week with him.

"Thanks," she managed, "but I think I'll watch the storm for little longer, then go to bed."

"No problem. If you change your mind, you know where to find me."

She smiled. "Thanks. Good night."

After Rosa left, she sat in the window seat for a while longer, feeling more alone than she had in a long, long time.

She awoke to absolute darkness and the strange, disorienting awareness that she didn't know where she was.

She blinked, aware of cold and wind and the faint hint of roses hanging on the air.

Was that what had awakened her? She blinked again as the sunroom of her apartment at Brambleberry House slowly came into focus. She was still curled up on the window seat, a blanket casually tossed over her. Her back ached from the odd position and her foot tingled, asleep.

She must have drifted off while watching the storm. She wasn't sure how she could have slept in the midst of the weather's intensity. Wind whined outside, fiercely hurling raindrops at the window.

Her phone suddenly rang and she had the feeling it wasn't the first time. It wasn't an alarm, but someone calling.

Skye!

Still trying to push away the tangled remnants of sleep, she scrambled for her phone and found it glowing under the throw blanket she must have tugged over her in the night.

"Hello?" She hardly recognized her own raspy voice.

"Melissa? Is that you?"

"I… Yes."

Not Skye, and not Cody. Some of her anxiety eased and she pulled the blanket tighter around her shoulders against the chill of the night and the storm.

"It's Julia Garrett. I'm so sorry to bother you, but I tried to call the clinic's emergency number and the phone lines must be down. I didn't have Eli's cell number and thought you might."

Her friend's words seemed to push away the last vestiges of sleep, and Melissa came fully awake. A hundred grim scenarios flashed through her head. It must be something serious for Julia to reach out at 1:00 a.m. in the middle of a storm.

"Are you all right? Is it one of the kids?"

"In a manner of speaking." Was that amusement she heard in Julia's voice? It hardly seemed appropriate, given the circumstances.

"I'm in labor."

Shock washed over her. "In labor. Now? Are you sure? Your cervix was only dilated to a one, eight hours ago when you left the office!"

"I've done this enough times, I'm pretty positive. I've had contractions all evening. I thought they were only Braxton Hicks, but in the past hour they've become much more regular."

"How far apart?"

"I'm down to about three minutes now."

Some of her wild panic subsided and she relaxed a little. "Okay. That's good. There's still time to make it to the hospital in Seaside."

"We thought so, too, but there's a problem. That's why I'm calling you. We were packing up the car and Will heard on the radio that the road is closed. The storm has knocked several big trees and power lines down between here and there."

Her voice cracked on the last word, and she started to breath heavily and regularly into the phone, obviously in the middle of a contraction. Melissa was already looking for her shoes by the door.

"That one was less than three minutes."

A new voice spoke into the phone. Julia must have handed the phone to her husband. Will was usually one of the most calm, measured people Melissa knew, but now he spoke briskly, his voice edged with the beginnings of panic. "I'm not sure what to do. Should I call for medevac?"

She wasn't at all prepared to make this sort of decision for the couple. "Let me call Eli and Wendell and see what they suggest. You told me you had a completely natural childbirth with your two youngest, with no complications. Eli may want to just have you meet us at the office."

"The only problem," Will said, "is that one of the downed power lines I heard about is apparently blocking the road between our place and Doc Sanderson's office. The only way I could figure out to get there is to walk, which I don't feel good about in this wind and storm, or to head down the beach on the four-wheeler."

"We're not doing either of those things," she heard Julia declare.

"Stay put," she said, shoving on her raincoat and her boots. "I'm on my way. I'll be there in five minutes. I'll get in touch with Eli and see if we can come up with a plan. If I can't get through, I'll stop and bang on his windows until he wakes up. Meanwhile, breathe, both of you. And don't let her have that baby yet."

"I'll do my best, but you know Jules. She can be pretty stubborn," Will said.

"I heard that," Melissa heard Julia say in the background.

Despite her own efforts to grab a flashlight and rush

out the door, Melissa had to fight a smile. Will and Julia were a darling couple, overflowing with love for each other and their children. She adored both of them.

"Hang tight. I'll be there in a few minutes."

"Be careful," Will said. "It's still pretty nasty out there. I don't like the idea of you going out in it, either."

"I won't let a little rain stop me," she assured him. "See you soon."

She hung up the phone as a particularly strong gust of wind rattled the windows of the old house.

She wasn't eager to go out into the teeth of the storm, but she also wasn't about to let her friend down. Not when Julia needed her.

He was having a delicious dream.

He and Melissa were walking through one of the dense ancient forests around Cannon Beach, her hand tucked in his. She carried a blanket in rich jewel tones and wore a sundress the same green as her eyes. Dappled light shot through the trees, catching in her hair.

She pulled her hand from his and raced ahead a little, turning around to look at him with that laughing, teasing smile that always stole his breath. He caught up with her and she wrapped her arms around his waist, pulling him close, where he was safe and warm and loved.

It was magic here, with a peace he hadn't known in months. He wanted to stay forever.

His phone jerked him awake and for an instant he was back in his residency, surviving on energy bars and rare, haphazard chunks of sleep.

He fumbled for it. "Hello?

"Eli. It's Melissa."

The discord of hearing the woman who had just been holding him in his dreams jarred him. Unlike the relaxed, warm woman he'd been dreaming about, her voice was strained and she pitched her voice above howling wind.

That same storm howled outside his father's house. He had been sitting in his dad's old recliner awake most of the night but must have eventually drifted off. He had a feeling he hadn't been sleeping long.

Eli sat up, his surroundings coming sharply back into focus. Melissa was calling and she needed him.

"What is it? What's wrong? Are you hurt?"

"I'm not hurt. I'm fine. But Julia Garrett is in labor and apparently the storm has blocked the road between here and Seaside, as well as between her house and the clinic."

"She was barely dilated this afternoon!"

"Tell that to her baby. Apparently it's on its own schedule. Now she's having contractions that are less than three minutes apart. I'm heading to their place now."

"In this storm?" Fear for her washed over him like a twenty-foot-high swell. Anything could happen to her. She could get hit by flying debris, stumble into a downed power line, fall and injure herself in the deep, powerless darkness.

He couldn't lose her!

"I'm fine. She needs help. Can you meet me there?"

He was already throwing on his shoes. "I only need five minutes. Be careful!"

"I know. Same to you."

She hung up before he could argue with her and tell her to go back inside Brambleberry House, where she would be safe.

"What's happening?"

In the light of a lantern, Wendell stood in the doorway, holding on to the walker he detested but still needed for stability. His father's hair was messy, and in his flannel pajamas he looked his age.

"I'm sorry I woke you. Julia Garrett's in labor, and apparently power lines are down between here and the hospital in Seaside."

"You didn't wake me. I can never sleep through storms like this. I've been in here fretting, wondering how long it would be before someone called, needing help. I didn't expect it to be Julia. She's three weeks from her due date."

He wasn't surprised that his father knew exactly when Julia was due, despite the fact that Wendell had been dealing with his own health issues and subsequent recovery for weeks.

"It was actually Melissa. Julia called her first and she was letting me know what was going on. Melissa is on her way over there and I'm going to meet her."

"She shouldn't be out in the storm, but you and I both know we can't stop her, especially since Julia is a friend of hers."

"We just saw Julia in the office yesterday. She was barely dilated, but of course babies have their own opinions about when they're going to make an appearance."

"Oh, yes. They love showing up when it's least convenient for anyone. You can take my emergency kit if you need it. I already pulled it out earlier in the evening and set it by the door. It should have everything you need."

He had his own emergency kit he kept stocked with supplies in a backpack, but he was touched his father had survived enough storms around Cannon Beach to make sure Eli, as his designated representative, was ready for anything.

"Thanks. I'll keep you posted."

"Take care of Julia. I know you will. You're an amazing doctor."

He wasn't as convinced, but his father's vote of confidence warmed him through. "I'll try."

"And take care of Melissa, too. She shouldn't be out in this storm."

"Exactly what I told her," he said. He didn't have time to tell his father how very much he yearned to take care of Melissa forever, to walk through all the storms of life together.

He grabbed his father's case and his own backpack, and headed out into the wind and lashing rain.

Melissa somehow beat him to the Garretts' house, but he suspected she hadn't been there long. Her hair was drenched, despite the raincoat she was taking off, and she looked cold.

He wanted to kiss the raindrops off her cheeks and hold her close to warm her up but knew both of them needed to focus on the crisis at hand.

"Thank you both for coming out in this crazy weather," Will Garrett said as he let Eli inside. "I'm sorry we had to call you in the middle of the night, but when we heard the roads were closed, we weren't sure what else to do."

"You did the right thing," Eli assured him.

"Trust Julia to make things more exciting," he said ruefully. "She's never content with the ordinary."

"You'll have a great story to tell this little one," Melissa said, her voice calm. She had so many strengths, but that was one he appreciated most: the calm that seemed to radiate from her.

"How do you have lights?" she asked.

"We have a whole-house generator. I put it in a few years ago. Believe me, I've never been so grateful for anything in my life," Will said gruffly.

When Eli pushed the door open, Melissa close behind him, they found Julia Garrett, dressed in a pale blue nightgown, sitting on the edge of the bed. A pretty teenage girl who had to be one of her twins sat next to her.

"Hey, Julia. Hi, Maddie." Melissa greeted both of them with more of that calm.

Julia managed a smile in response though her features were taut and strained. "This isn't quite the way I planned this."

"What is it with babies, deciding to make their appearances in the middle of the night in the worst possible weather?"

"Inconsiderate little stinks, aren't they?"

She smiled at them and then caught her breath, pressing both hands over her abdomen.

"That one was barely a minute since the last one," Maddie said, eyes huge and frightened in her pretty face.

"We're okay," Julia said, reaching out a hand to give

her daughter's arm a reassuring squeeze. "The cavalry is here now. You and Will won't have to deliver your baby sister."

"Whew," the girl said, vast relief on her face.

Eli considered his options quickly. "How do you feel about a home birth? I don't think we have time to call the air ambulance and have them here in time for the delivery, and I'm not sure they can fly in this wind anyway. We can have them on standby in case there any complications."

"Women have been giving birth at home forever," Julia said. "As long as she's safe, I don't care how she gets here."

He had plenty of colleagues who would have disagreed and would have insisted a hospital was the only safe place for a woman to give birth, but Eli's experience in war zones and refugee camps had told him that women could be incredibly resourceful. Under the circumstances, this was the safest possible place for Julia to have her baby, not in a helicopter or an ambulance trying to make its way through the storm.

Even if they had called for a chopper, it turned out that Julia's labor progressed so quickly it was clear it wouldn't have arrived in time. He and Melissa barely had time to arrange her on the bed, put a nervous Will at ease and send Maddie for clean towels and to boil water to sterilize any tools he needed to use.

Ten minutes later, he watched a head emerge.

Sweat poured down Julia's face and she gripped her husband's hand tightly. "I have to push."

"That's good," Eli said. "I need you to do just that. Now is the perfect time to push. You've got this."

A moment later, he delivered a chunky, red-faced baby, who took a shuddering breath, then began to wail.

"Love that sound," Melissa said, wiping off the baby's face with an awestruck expression. "Welcome to the world, little Garrett girl."

"Miriam Renee," Will said, his voice raw with emotions. "We want to call her Miri."

Eli caught his breath. It was a coincidence, he knew, but hearing the name out of the blue like that still made him feel as if he'd been run over by a tank.

For a moment he was frozen, picturing a sweet girl, bloodied and torn, her smile cut down forever by hatred and violence. A strangled cry choked him and he couldn't breathe or think. He had to get out of here before the memories consumed him and he fell apart. In a panic, his muscles tensed and he was about to rise, to escape, when he felt the gentle pressure of fingers on his shoulder.

Melissa.

His gaze met hers, and he saw a knowledge and compassion there that made him swallow back the emotions. She knew. She knew and somehow she steadied him. He had no idea how she managed it. He only knew that the warm touch of her hand on him seemed to clear away the panic and the grief and shock until he felt much more in control.

He drew in a shuddering breath and cleared his throat. "Miri is a beautiful name for a beautiful little girl."

"She's gorgeous," Will said gruffly. "Like her mother."

He kissed Julia's sweat-dampened forehead, running a tender hand down her hair. After Eli helped Will cut the cord with the sterilized scissors he had in his kit, Melissa took the baby and placed the naked, wriggling girl on Julia's chest. She instinctively rooted around, and Julia laughed a little before helping her latch on. Will stood next to them, his somewhat harsh features relaxed into an expression of love and amazement and a vast joy.

"Good job, Mama," Eli said.

His voice sounded ragged but he didn't care. He had delivered babies before, into the hundreds, but he couldn't remember when a birth had impacted him so deeply.

He was emotional about Miri but about so much more. He wanted this, what Will and Julia had created here. A family.

He had seen so much ugliness over the last five years of near-constant deployments. Pain and bloodshed and violence. Families torn apart, villages decimated, lives shattered.

All of it stemmed from hatred, from power struggles and greed and ideological differences.

He was so tired of it.

Maybe it was time he focused instead on love.

He had been doing important work overseas, helping people in terrible situations who had few options and little hope. He couldn't deny that what he had been doing *mattered.*

Justine had been doing important work, and some part of him would always feel a responsibility to try harder and be better because of her example and the tragic way she had died.

But this was important, too, these small but significant moments. Helping to bring new life into the world. Caring for neighbors and friends. Continuing his father's legacy in this community, where Wendell was so loved.

"Are you all right?" Melissa asked a short time later, after the baby was bundled and the ambulance had been called. Both mom and baby were fine, but as soon as the road was cleared, Eli wanted them to be checked out at the hospital, where little Miri could have a full assessment and Julia could receive care while she recovered.

He wanted to tell her some of the many thoughts racing through his head, but now didn't seem the proper time.

"I'm fine. It's always amazing, seeing new life come into the world and remembering what a miracle it is, every time. I heard it said once that a baby is God's opinion that the world should go on. I think I needed that reminder."

Her features softened and she touched his arm again. The tenderness of the gesture made those emotions well up.

He was so deeply in love with her. How had he ever been crazy enough to think he could go on without her?

"I didn't know about the name. They were still trying to decide, the last I talked to Julia about it. If I had known, I would have warned you."

"It's a lovely name," he said. "I hope she's as sweet as the other little girl I once knew who carried it."

Before she could answer, Eli's phone rang. When he saw his father on the caller ID, he quickly answered it.

"Hey, son," Wendell said. "How are things going there? How's Julia?"

"Good. Both the mama and baby girl are doing fine."

"Oh, that's wonderful to hear. I knew you could do it."

His father's confidence in him warmed him. "Right now we're waiting for the road to open so we can get them to the hospital in Seaside. The crews are saying about another half hour."

"Great news. Listen, I just got a call from Elisa Darby. A branch came through her teenage boy's bedroom window about a half hour ago."

"Oh, no!"

"He's fine, just shaken up, but might need a couple of stitches. It's not a big deal, not big enough to try getting to the ER in Seaside in this storm, but she called to see if someone could come by, check things out and maybe stitch him up. You up for another house call?"

He assessed the situation with the Garretts. Will and Julia had things under control. Right now, their teenage daughter was holding the bundled baby and her siblings were waiting in line for their turn.

"I can do that. Text me the address. I'll wrap up with Julia and head there within the next fifteen or twenty minutes."

"If other people call, want me to start making a list? I can be your dispatcher."

"Sure."

He hung up from his father to find Julia watching carefully. "What's happened?"

"I've got a teenage boy with an injury from broken glass after a branch came through a window."

"I was worried about that very thing happening to me earlier. I fell asleep in the window seat while I was watching the storm and woke up thinking it probably wasn't a good idea."

"It wasn't. You should probably not do that again." He wanted to be here to hold her during the next storm. The two of them could keep each other warm and watch the clouds roll over the ocean together.

"Where did it happen?" she asked.

"The house of Elisa Darby. Do you know her?"

"Yes. She doesn't live far from here.

"Apparently, her son might need a few stitches."

"You'll need help."

To give someone stitches? Probably not. He'd been doing that since his first day of med school, but he couldn't deny the two of them made a good team. She seemed to know exactly what supplies he needed without being asked, and he definitely needed her amazing skill at calming any situation.

"I don't want to take you away if you think you're still needed here."

Will glanced over, obviously listening to the conversation. "We're fine. The ambulance should be here soon. You've done great work and I can't thank you enough for our little Miri here, but it sounds like somebody else needs you now."

"If you're sure."

Melissa seemed reluctant to leave, but she gathered up their supplies, gave Julia a kiss on the cheek and hugged

Will. Then she kissed the baby's forehead before following Eli out into the pearly light of predawn.

The wind had finally slowed, though the rain continued. The sun was still an hour or so from coming up above the mountains to the east, but there was enough light for them to see some of the damage left behind by the storm.

On this street alone, nearly every house had at least one tree branch down, and he could see a metal shed collapsed at the Garretts' neighbors. This was only one small sample of what the storm could do. He had a feeling the rest of the region had been hit just as hard.

He met Melissa's gaze. "I have a feeling it's going to be a busy day."

Chapter Eleven

Eli's words turned out to be prophetic. By the time they finished at the Darbys' house, Wendell had called them to report three more people had phoned him looking for emergency medical care. They all had mild cuts and bruises, except for one man who sustained minor burns trying to start a malfunctioning generator. Eli patched him up as best he could but ordered him to the hospital as soon as he could make it there.

They made house calls at first, but as they started to receive reports that the roads were slowly being cleared throughout the morning, he and Melissa were finally able to retreat to the clinic, sending out word to the real dispatchers and the paramedics that they would stay open to take some of the more mild emergencies where a trip to the hospital wasn't necessarily warranted.

She loved seeing Eli in action during a crisis. Over the last three weeks during routine office visits, she had observed that he was truly a wonderful doctor, one who spent as much time as each patient needed, dispensing advice and compassion.

Observing him during an emergency situation was something completely different. He was focused, concise, with an uncanny ability to take care of whatever situation walked through the door with skill and care.

No wonder he was so passionate about his military career. Eli was a man who truly thrived under pressure.

She couldn't expect someone with a gift like that to be content as a family physician in a small practice.

The realization depressed her, though she was not sure why. Maybe she had been holding out some slim hope that Eli might be able to find a place to belong here on the beautiful Oregon Coast where he had been raised, exactly as *she* had over the last seven months.

Around noon, she closed the outside doors after their last patient, a tearful eight-year-old girl who had stepped on a nail while helping her family clean up debris. When the family drove away, no cars were left in the parking lot. She locked the doors and turned the Open sign to Closed.

At last report, the dispatchers assured them all the roads were clear now along the coast and people in need could make it to the emergency room or the urgent-care clinics in Seaside or Astoria, if necessary.

"Good work," Eli said when she walked back. "You've been amazing today. An army medic trained in battlefield emergency care couldn't have done better."

His admiring words and expression left her flustered and not sure how to respond. "You were the one doing all the care. I've only been providing support."

"That's completely not true and you know it. Every time I needed something, you were right there with it before I had to ask, and you are amazing at calming down every panicked mother or crying child."

"We make a good team." For another week, anyway. The thought made her chest ache.

"Do you have any idea of how necessary you are to my father's practice? Why do you think I've tried so hard to..." He bit off his words, leaving her intensely curious about what he intended to say.

"Why you've tried so hard to what?" She had to ask.

His smile appeared forced. "Uh, make sure you know exactly how much you're appreciated."

She had a feeling that wasn't what he'd almost said at all, but he didn't appear inclined to add anything more.

"I was going to say the same to you," she said. "It's not every day you deliver a baby, sew thirty-six stitches in five different patients and give eight tetanus shots, all before noon."

He smiled. "All in all, a good morning. I'm glad we could help."

"If you hadn't been here, I'm not sure what people in Cannon Beach would have done."

"My dad is not the only doctor in town. Someone else would have stepped up."

Wendell might not be the only doctor, but he was one of the most beloved.

Eli was well on his way to matching his father's popularity. Everyone in town loved Eli, after he had been here only three weeks to fill in for his father.

Especially her.

She pushed the thought aside. Not now. She couldn't think about her impending heartache. He was leaving in a week, and somehow she was going to have to figure out how to go on without that slow, gorgeous smile in her life.

She had to say at least a little of what was on her mind. It seemed vitally important that she let him know what she had been thinking all morning as she watched him work.

"You're an amazing doctor, Eli. You make a great family physician in the proud tradition of your father, but today, working together in an emergency situation with you, showed me you're doing exactly what you need to be doing for the army. You obviously thrive in stressful situations. You care passionately about what you're doing and you're good at it—exactly the sort of person who can make a much-needed difference in the world."

He looked touched, his eyes warm, and he opened his mouth to answer, but his cell phone rang before he could say anything. He gave the phone a frustrated look that shifted to one of concern when he saw the caller ID.

"I need to get that. Looks like it's the Seaside hospital, probably the attending physician at the women's center, calling about Julia and Miri."

"While you talk to the Attending, I'll go straighten up the exam rooms we used today so they're ready for Monday."

She was just finishing up when Eli appeared in the

doorway, again looking dark and lean and so gorgeous it made her catch her breath.

"Mom and baby are doing well," he reported. "I figured you'd want to know."

"Yes. I was going to call her later. I appreciate the update."

"Everyone is healthy. The attending physician suggests keeping them overnight, but it sounds like Julia is eager to be home with their other children. I'll go check things out, and if all appears okay she might be released by tonight."

"She'll be happy about that."

He leaned against the door frame and scratched his cheek. "Better yet, I'll pick up my dad and take him with me to do the honors. He'll want to see the baby and check on Julia himself."

Her heart melted at his thoughtfulness, both on his father's behalf and on Julia's, and she fell in love with him all over again.

"You are a good man, Eli Sanderson."

He made a face. "Why? Because I'm going to take my dad with me to the hospital to check on a patient?"

"Because you know how important it is for him to make sure she's all right and also how much it will set Julia's mind at ease to have him there."

"It's not a big deal."

"It is to me, just as it will be for Julia and your dad."

She smiled at him, and he gazed at her for a long moment, then growled something she couldn't hear and lowered his mouth to hers.

The fierce kiss came out of the blue and was the last

thing she expected him to do, yet somehow was exactly what she needed.

His mouth was hard and intense on hers, searching and demanding at the same time. She answered him kiss for kiss, taste for taste. Heat raced through her and she wrapped her arms around him, but the hunger contained something else, something deeper.

This was goodbye.

He was leaving in a week, and this likely would be the last chance she would have to hold him like this before he left. She tightened her arms, trying to burn the taste and the feel and the smell of him into her mind. When he was gone, back doing the work he loved, and she was alone here in Cannon Beach, at least she would have these slices of memories to comfort her.

She tried to pour everything in her heart into the kiss. All her love and admiration and sadness, wrapped together and delivered on a breathless sigh. She had no idea how long they stayed locked together there in the doorway. She only knew the emotions in the kiss would leave her forever changed.

She would have stayed forever, but she was aware, always aware, that someone else needed him, too.

After long, heady moments, she finally pulled her mouth away and stepped back, her breathing ragged and her face flaming. Could he sense in her kiss all the love she couldn't say?

She looked away, hoping desperately that she hadn't revealed entirely too much by that kiss.

"Melissa."

His voice sounded raw, breathless. She could feel his

searching gaze on her and forced herself to offer back a bland smile. "You should probably go check out Julia and Miri. The Garretts will be waiting for you."

"I… Yes."

She didn't want him to offer any explanations or apologies or, worse, ask any questions. Any conversation between them and she was afraid she would burst into tears she couldn't explain.

"I'll see you later. Drive carefully."

With that, she turned around and hurried out of the room, wishing with all her heart that things could be different between them.

Though she was tired down to her bones, Melissa spent the afternoon working with Sonia to clean up the battered gardens at Brambleberry House. Rosa was busy doing the same at the gift store in town, which had suffered some water damage from a roof leak.

The gardens looked sad, with broken limbs, crushed flowers, scattered leaves.

She felt a little like the landscaping around the house—damaged, scarred. She had to hope she could be like a few of the shrubs around the house, which had been bent by the storm but were already beginning to straighten again.

"I don't think we can save this one." Sonia sat before one of the brambleberry bushes, her lovely, perfect features creased with a grief that seemed out of proportion to a little storm damage.

"Are you sure we can't salvage some of the canes?"

"They won't be the same. I'm not sure they'll be able to produce much fruit at all."

She seemed devastated by the loss. Maybe she had an extreme fondness for that particular brambleberry bush, or maybe her grief was for something else entirely.

Melissa tried to choose her words carefully. "You know, my dad used to say that not everything that's broken is worthless. It might not ever be what it was, but that doesn't mean it can't be something else. Maybe something even better."

She wasn't sure if she had helped or made things worse. Sonia gave her a long look, nodded slowly, then went back to work.

"That's all we can do tonight," Sonia said sometime later. "It's going to be dark soon. You look very tired. You need to rest."

Her exhaustion had deepened, and she thought she might fall asleep right here in the cool, storm-battered garden.

"I'll just stay with Fiona for a moment, then we'll come inside."

Sonia gave her a long look and she could see the concern on her friend's features. She didn't pry, though. One of the best things about Sonia was her ability to let other people keep their own secrets, too. After a moment, the other woman twisted her mouth into what other people might consider a smile and headed into the house.

Melissa sat for a few moments more, heart aching. She needed to go inside but couldn't seem to find the energy to do it.

She wanted her daughter here. A Skye hug always went a long way toward healing her soul from life's inevitable disappointments. Her daughter would be home the next day. They would have plenty of time for hugs then.

She was just about to head into the house when Fiona suddenly turned around and raced for the edge of the garden.

What on earth?

"Fiona," she called. "Come on, girl. Home."

The dog ignored her, headed with single-minded purpose in the other direction. There was probably some poor mole who had been foolish enough to set up shop in the gardens the Irish setter considered her own.

Fiona didn't stop when she reached the beach access gate. To Melissa's astonishment, she nudged open the latch and raced through, leaving her little choice but to chase after the dog.

She was too tired for this, but Fiona didn't seem to care about that.

Exasperated, Melissa followed the dog onto the beach. "Come on, Fi. Here girl," she called, then her voice faltered.

Fiona wasn't alone. She stood on the sand not far from the house, nose to nose with another dog. A little black schnauzer, whose leash was currently held by the one man she didn't feel strong enough to face again right now.

Her heart seemed to stutter, and she wanted to slip back through the gate and hurry into the house.

After that emotional kiss earlier when she had bared everything in her heart, she didn't want to face him right now…or ever again, if she could arrange it.

But he was here and she had no choice. She forced

herself to move toward him. "Sorry. She got out somehow. Come on, Fiona. Inside."

The dog showed no sign of obeying her, and Melissa sighed, taking another step toward him and the two dogs.

"Julia and Will send their love and gratitude," he said when she was an arm's length away.

Despite her discomfort, she couldn't help a smile at that. "How is Julia? I wanted to go visit but thought I would give her a day or two to be settled at home."

"She's good. Glowing."

That made her smile again. "And baby Miri?"

"Beautiful. I held her for a good fifteen minutes while the infant unit nurses were giving me their report and she slept the whole time. She obviously likes me."

Why wouldn't she? The man was irresistible. Her heart ached when she pictured him in a hospital nursery, holding a tiny baby who shared the same name as someone dear to him, someone he had lost.

She was suddenly deeply grateful she would have the chance to watch this Miri grow up. She would be here to see her learn to walk, to ride a bike, to go on dates. Melissa, at least, wasn't going anywhere.

"Maybe Julia can keep in touch with you after you're back on active duty and send you pictures of her."

He was quiet, his hands on Max's leash. "That would be great, except I'm not going back on active duty."

She stared at him in the gathering twilight. "You're… what?"

He returned her shocked look with an impassive one she couldn't read. "I called my commanding officer on my way back from the hospital and told her I wouldn't be signing up for another tour."

"But…but why? I thought you loved what you do in the military. You were doing important work. Necessary work."

"I am. I was. But today when we were delivering Miri, I realized something."

He gazed toward the ocean and the dramatic rock formations offshore, his features in shadow.

"There is more than one way to make a difference in the world," he said slowly. "Sometimes that involves focusing on helping out those in critical situations. That's a good and honorable thing to do, and I will always be grateful I had the experiences and learned the lessons I did."

He glanced back at her, blue eyes glittering in the fading light. "I'm glad I had the chance to serve. I'm a better doctor and a better person for it. But I have no obligation to do it forever. Even Justine was never planning to serve for the rest of her life. She was making plans for after she left Doctors Without Borders. She was going to adopt Miri and take her back to France with her."

"Yes. That's what you said."

"If she could make plans for a different future someday, why can't I?"

"What kind of future?" Her heart now seemed to be racing in double time as she tried to absorb this shocking information.

"I want to be home. I want to help my neighbors and be around when my dad needs me and watch Miri and any other babies I deliver grow up and have babies of their own."

"You're leaving the army." She couldn't seem to process it even after his explanation.

He shrugged. "I'm leaving active duty. I'll stay in the reserves. If my country needs me, I may end up being called up in emergencies. I'm more than willing to do that on a temporary basis, but I want something else. I want to go into practice with my dad. Sanderson and Sanderson. Has a nice ring, don't you think?"

Oh, that would make Wendell happy beyond words. "Your dad will be thrilled."

"He will. With me here to share the burden, who knows? He might even slow down and little and start to enjoy life outside of medicine."

She wasn't sure that would happen, but she hoped so for his father's sake.

As she processed the news, the magnitude of what he was telling her began to soak through her shock. He was staying in Cannon Beach. Staying at the clinic where she worked. That would only mean one thing.

She would have no choice.

"That's great. I'm happy for you. You'll be gr-great."

Tears began to burn behind her eyes, and she had to hope he couldn't see them in the dusky light.

Unfortunately, she forgot how sharp-eyed the man could be. His gaze narrowed and he watched her with an intensity she couldn't escape.

"What's wrong? I was hoping for a...different reaction."

"I'm happy for you. I really am. This is exactly what your father would have wanted."

"So why do you look like I just started clear-cutting the Brambleberry House gardens?"

She wanted to come up with something clever that would explain the tears she was afraid he had seen, but she was too tired to tell him anything but the truth.

"I love working at your dad's practice," she said softly. "But if you're coming home for good, I'm afraid I'll have to quit."

His mouth sagged. "Quit? Why the hell would you do that?"

She had to tell him, especially now that she'd started. The words caught in her throat, but she forced them out.

"I can't work for you, Eli. I can't. Not when I…" She faltered, losing her nerve.

He looked thunderstruck, as if she'd just thrown a handful of sand in his eyes. "When you what?"

She closed her eyes, mortified to her soul that she'd said anything at all. She should have just let the dust settle for a week or so and then quietly tendered her resignation.

"Are you really going to make me say it? Fine. I'll say it, then. I can't work for you when I have…have feelings for you."

This was the most difficult conversation she'd ever had. She wanted to find a hole and let Fiona and Max bury her in it like a leftover soup bone.

"These last two weeks have been torture," she finally admitted, "trying to keep things on a professional level when my heart wants so much more. I'm sorry. I can't do it. I'm not strong enough. I'll have to go somewhere else to work. I'm sure I can find another job somewhere else along the coast. I only hope your dad will be able to give me a good reference."

He didn't say anything for a full minute, his expression filled with shock and something else, something she couldn't identify.

"Say something," she finally couldn't help but say.

When he continued to stare at her, she grabbed Fiona's collar and turned to head to the house, wanting only to escape.

"Melissa. Stop. Please!"

Fiona plopped her hindquarters in the sand, refusing to move other step, while a warm, rose-scented breeze seemed to eddy around them.

She couldn't face him. Humiliated and miserable, she stood there outside the beach gate, not knowing what to do.

She thought she knew what love was. She had been married for five years, for heaven's sake. But everything she understood before seemed wholly insignificant compared to this vast ache of emotion coiling through her.

"Melissa."

He tugged her around to face him, and she finally slowly lifted her gaze to his. The emotions blazing there made her catch her breath. Her pulse in her ears seemed louder than the surf.

"I want to stay in Cannon Beach for dozens of reasons," he said, his voice low and intense. "And almost every single one of them is because of you."

She gazed at his strong, lean features, everything inside her tuned to this moment.

"I came back to town broken," he went on gruffly. "I didn't want to admit it to myself or anyone else, but something inside my head and heart shattered when Miri and Justine died. I wouldn't say it was post-traumatic stress disorder, but the whole world seemed empty, joyless. Wrong."

He smiled a little and reached for her hand. His skin was warm against hers, and she shivered at the contrast, wanting to lean into him but afraid to move.

"And then I came back to town and met up with the girl I had the biggest crush on when I was eighteen and she was just fifteen, and I started to heal."

"You did not have a crush on me."

He raised an eyebrow. "Do you remember that time we danced together at the prom? Your boyfriend tried to beat me up later, but I didn't care. I would have done it all over again. It was all worth it, for the few moments I got to hold you in my arms."

"Why didn't you say anything? Back then or now?"

"You were way out of my league back then. You still are. I know I'll never be good enough for you, but that doesn't seem to matter anymore. The only thing that matters is that I'm in love with you and want the chance to show you I can make you happy."

Joy exploded through her, fierce and bright and perfect. "You love me."

"I think I've loved you a little since we were in high school together. But when I came back to Cannon Beach and met you again—the strong, amazing, compassionate woman you've become—I fell in love all over again."

Warmth flowed over her, healing and blissful. He loved her. She would never get tired of those words.

She reached up on tiptoe and kissed him, and this time when his mouth met hers there were no reservations between them, no uneasiness or worry or doubts.

Only love.

He kissed her for a long time, until the sun had almost slipped into the ocean. She would never grow tired of his kisses, either.

"I love you, Elias Sanderson. I'm so in love with you, I've barely been able to function around you. I'm amazed I could do my job, I was so busy trying to hide my feelings about you."

"Whatever you did worked. I had no idea."

She wanted to laugh and dance barefoot in the sand and fly a hundred kites with hearts all over them. Joy soared through her, wild and fierce and perfect.

He wouldn't be returning to harm's way. He would be here in Cannon Beach with her where they could walk the dogs at sunset and teach Skye how to play billiards and listen to music at The Haystacks on Saturday nights.

They could work together, helping the neighbors and friends they cared about.

Storms would come. Tree limbs would fall and brambleberry bushes would be broken and torn. But they would get through it all together.

He kissed her, and that future seemed sweet and full of incalculable promise.

"I'm not that young, perky cheerleader anymore,"

she eventually felt compelled to remind him when his hands started to wander.

"I know," he murmured against her mouth. "You're so much more than that now. A loving mother, a compassionate nurse, a loyal friend. And the woman who has my heart."

She could live with that.

She smiled and kissed him as a warm, rose-scented breeze danced around them like an embrace.

Epilogue

Humming one of her favorite Christmas songs, Rosa Galvez twisted another string of lights around one of the porch columns. She only had two more to go, then this part of her holiday decorating would be done.

She loved this time of year. Brambleberry House was at its most beautiful at Christmas. The old Victorian was made for the season. Wreaths hung on the front door and in every window and her neighbor Sonia had been busy for the past two weeks hanging lights around the garden. Well, busy supervising a crew of teenage neighbor boys, anyway, who were earning a little extra change while helping them decorate.

The house would be spectacular when they finished.

She twisted the last of the strand of lights around the

column, grateful for her coat against the cool, damp afternoon.

Though it was barely December, a Christmas tree already gleamed in the window of the first-floor apartment and she could see Skye peeking out. The girl waved at Rosa and at Fiona, sprawled out on the porch watching her work, then disappeared from view, back inside where she was baking something with Melissa.

Rosa had to smile, though she felt a little pang in her heart. The house would seem so empty when Skye and her mother moved out, but at least she wouldn't have to worry about that for a few more months. Eli Sanderson and Melissa Fielding planned to marry here at Brambleberry House in April, when the flowers were first beginning to bloom in the gardens. It would be a lovely place to marry. She wanted to think Abigail would have been happy at the romantic turn of events.

Melissa and Eli were already looking at houses and seemed to have found a lovely Craftsman home close to Wendell Sanderson's house.

She was happy for her friend but, oh, she would miss her and Skye. So would Fiona. Who was going to take the Irish setter on runs along the shore? Certainly not Rosa.

She was hanging the last of the lights when a big late-model pickup truck she didn't recognize pulled into the driveway and a tall, serious-looking man climbed out. He stood for a moment, looking up at the house, then walked toward her.

For reasons she couldn't have explained, Rosa tensed. She hardly ever had the panic attacks and meltdowns that had afflicted her so much after the dark period of her youth, before she had been rescued by Sheriff Daniel Galvez and his wife, Lauren, who later adopted her. Those terrible months seemed a lifetime ago. She was a different person now, one who had worked hard to find happiness.

Every once in a while, she felt as if all the progress she had achieved over the last fifteen years was for nothing—that somewhere deep inside, she would always be a frightened girl, tangled in a situation out of her control.

"May I help you?" she asked as the man approached the porch.

"I hope so."

Up close, he seemed even more grim than he had appeared when he climbed out of his vehicle. No trace of a smile appeared on his features, only tight control.

"I'm looking for a woman. I'm pretty sure she lives here. Her name is Elizabeth Hamilton."

The name meant nothing to Rosa, who knew all the past tenants going back to the original owner. Still, she felt a stirring of unease.

"I know no one by this name," she said. She was nervous, which was probably the reason that her Spanish accent became more pronounced. "I believe you have the wrong house."

"It's not the wrong house," he said flatly. "I know she's here."

"And I know she is not," Rosa retorted. Like her accent, her unease was becoming more pronounced, as well. This man made her nervous, though she couldn't have said why.

She wondered, for one fleeting moment, whether she should pull her phone out and call 911. It was a crazy reaction, she knew. The man wasn't threatening anyone. He was only looking for a woman who did not live there. She could only imagine trying to explain why she had called the police for such a reason to the frustrating but gorgeous new police chief. Wyatt Townsend would look at her with even more suspicion than he usually did.

"Now, I must ask you to leave."

She saw frustration cross features that she would ordinarily call handsome. Right now, they only looked dangerous.

"Sorry, ma'am, but I've come too far to leave now."

There was a bit of a Western twang to his voice, one that seemed similar to those she heard throughout her teenage years living in Utah.

"The woman you are seeking, this Elizabeth Hamilton, she does not live here."

He let out a sigh and looked down at the piece of paper. "What about Sonia Davis. Is she here?"

Now her nervousness bloomed into full-on fear. What could he possibly want with their Sonia?

Her neighbor was home. Rosa had seen her come in earlier and make her painstaking way up to her second-floor apartment, looking more weary and sore than usual.

She wanted to tell him no. She wanted to tell him to go away and not come back. Some instinct warned Rosa that this man was a threat to her secretive, vulnerable neighbor, who had already been through so very much.

She opened her mouth to lie but closed it again. What if Sonia was expecting him? What if she wanted to see this handsome man in cowboy boots and a worn ranch jacket, who drove a pickup truck that had Idaho license plates and the words Hamilton Construction on the side.

"She lives upstairs." She couldn't see any point in lying. He obviously knew Sonia lived here. "If you would like, I can see if she is home. What name should I tell her? And is there a message you would you like me to give her?"

He glanced up, almost as if he could see through the porch ceiling to the floor above. Now the tight expression showed a crack of emotion, something stark and raw. She thought she saw longing, frustration, pain, before his features became closed again.

"Sure. My name is Luke Hamilton. And you can tell this Sonia—whose real name, by the way, is Elizabeth Sinclair Hamilton—that her husband has come to take her home."

* * * * *

Watch for Luke and Elizabeth's story,
the next book in the Haven Point series,
available this September from HQN.

Rosa Galvez's story,
next in The Women of Brambleberry House series,
will be coming soon.